I0829330

HER Almost FIANCÉ Cowboy

KARAN BANEY

Her Almost Fiancé Cowboy (Love at Vargas Ranch Book 2)
By Karen Baney

Cover Design by Karen Baney

Publisher:
Desert Life Media, LLC
Gilbert, AZ 85295

www.karenbaney.com

Printed in the United States of America

ISBN- 978-1-960217-77-6

Do not remember the past events; pay no attention to things of old. Look, I am about to do something new; even now it is coming. Do you not see it? Indeed, I will make a way in the wilderness, rivers in the desert.

– Isaiah 43:18-19

1

"YOU'VE GOT THIS, Gregory. Drop to one knee. Say the words."

Cole stared at his reflection in the mirror, his stomach churning. The same pep talk he'd used on dozens of athletes did nothing to calm his nerves. Could have something to do with the four failed attempts over the last six months.

But tonight…

Tonight was Sydney's thirtieth birthday. He was taking her to Elements at the Sanctuary Camelback Mountain. A special date place. Like a proposal or anniversary place.

The reflection staring back at him frowned, lines forming across his forehead. He looked the part in his sleek charcoal gray Tom Ford jacket—Shelton fit. Deep blue button-down shirt, collar open. The dark indigo Tom Ford denim was a new look for him. Along with the Lucchese black cowboy boots and black Stetson—both must-haves according to his best friend and boss, Derin Vargas. A worthy outfit for a proposal if there ever was one.

Turning from the mirror, he stuffed two jewelry boxes in his pockets. Right ring. Left necklace. The bailout gift. Just in case. It was her birthday after all. He couldn't skip giving her something. And he couldn't leave the rental house without a back up plan.

Cole walked past the stack of unpacked boxes and eyed

the two sets of keys on the hook by the door. McLaren Spyder? Ram 1500 TRX? Both were impressive. And impractical for ranch life. But he wasn't a ranch hand, and he'd spent his first career as a sports agent to some big names in the NFL, MLB, and more. No wife. No kids. More money than he knew what to do with.

McLaren. Yeah. It was a special night and a long drive.

As he grabbed the keys and climbed behind the wheel, his phone pinged.

Instagram alert. *Don't look at it. Don't look at it.*

He looked at it.

Audrey.

His gut twisted at the picture. Her new husband, youth-pastor Jeff. Their three kids. A day at the beach looked picture-perfect.

And every bit of everything Cole had never been for her.

Tonight of all nights. Not good. He didn't need the reminder. Not if he hoped to seal the deal with Sydney.

Cole gripped the steering wheel tightly as images from a lifetime ago scrolled across his mind's eye. The echoes of heated arguments ringing in his ears. She'd wanted more from him. More than he could give. He was building his career. He'd been faithful. Came home as often as he could.

But building his career as a premier sports agent required more sacrifices than Audrey could accept.

He hadn't been enough.

Cole frowned and turned on loud Christian music to drown out the failures of his youth. He had to get in the right headspace. For Sydney.

The bass pounded through the speakers as he drove on the quiet streets of Forepaugh. Ten minutes to the ranch. Ten minutes to pull himself together.

Four times. He'd almost proposed four times over the last six months.

Christmas at the ranch. Twinkling lights. Friends gathered. The moment had been perfect. Until it wasn't.

Valentine's Day in Scottsdale. Romantic dinner. Roses. He'd reached for the ring box and... nothing.

That trail ride last month. Sunset at the overlook. Arizona desert painted gold and orange. Sydney's hand in his. The words stuck in his throat like concrete.

Some random Tuesday at work. They'd been alone in his office. She smiled at him, and everything felt right. Simple. True. Then his phone rang, and the moment vanished.

Four times he'd choked.

Tonight was attempt number five.

His phone buzzed in the cupholder. Text from Derin.

Tonight's the night, bro. Praying for you.

Cole stared at the screen. Derin didn't know. Didn't know about his past life. The fear that ate at him in the dark.

Another text.

Madison says if you don't propose tonight, she's staging an intervention.

Cole's lips twitched despite the knot in his stomach. Madison would too. She'd been dropping hints for months about Sydney's biological clock.

He should text back. Something confident.

Instead, he turned off the music. The silence pressed in.

The ring box sat in his right pocket. He'd carried it for six months. Round stone. Small diamonds trailing down each side. Simple, classic, and exactly her.

If he could just give it to her.

He hadn't been enough for Audrey. Wasn't sure he'd be enough for Sydney.

Cole shook his head. Sydney wasn't Audrey. He wasn't the same man he'd been back then. He'd changed. Grown.

Except the fear remained. Paralyzing. Suffocating.

Father, help me. Please. I want to do this. I need to do this.

The prayer felt weak. Inadequate.

The little convenience store came into view, and he eased off the gas. He stopped and bought a bouquet of mixed flowers. Red roses, white carnations, and a few pops of some yellow flower he didn't know the name of. Simple. Sweet.

Like Sydney.

His Sydney. Knockout redhead with an atypical personality. Kind. Compassionate. Loving.

That she loved him at all still surprised him most days.

"You can do this, Gregory," he said as he turned onto the gravel drive toward Vargas Ranch, the Spyder's hum sending a thrill through him. A fleeting reprieve from his thoughts.

Yet the doubt niggled, picking at his confidence like a scorpion sting. Didn't matter that Sydney wasn't Audrey. He hadn't been enough back then. Probably couldn't be now.

He slowed as he turned down the lane to the women's housing where his Sydney lived.

"Thirty is a big deal for women, Cole," Madison told him a few days ago. "Bio clock and all."

Cole knew that was her way of hinting that he'd better not fail this time. Madison's husband, Derin, had been infinitely more direct. "Put a ring on it, bro."

His cheeks puffed before he exhaled loudly.

A prayer hovered at the edge of his heart only to be swallowed by the Insta beach picture. He cut the engine and patted his left pocket, confirming the bailout gift was still there.

He probably shouldn't propose on her birthday, anyway. Her thirtieth birthday.

Her bio clock birthday.

Cole swallowed hard, snatching the insufficient bouquet from the passenger seat. He stepped out of the sports car and rapped his knuckles against Sydney's front door.

"Hey, Cole. Sydney's almost ready," Solana Vargas said as she swung the door open. "Oh, let me grab a vase for her."

He stepped over the threshold, scanning the familiar space. Sydney's room was on the left of the great room at the back of the apartment. Renata Vargas smiled a greeting from her perch on the overstuffed couch.

"Special occasion? You look great!" she exclaimed.

Heat climbed up his neck and face before settling in the tips of his ears.

Solana snorted. "Cole always brings the classy vibes."

Thankfully, Sydney emerged from her room just then. Words fled his mind at the sight of her creamy skin against a bright green dress. Her emerald eyes sparkled as her soft lips spread into a huge smile. Her long red hair hung in stunning waves. She looked gorgeous.

Cole cleared his throat as he held out one hand for hers and the flowers in the other. She clasped his hand and leaned forward, placing a light kiss on his lips, already off script from their routine cheek peck. His throat clogged as she reached for the bouquet.

"Thank you for the flowers." She lifted them to her nose and breathed in, those emerald gems glinting beneath her lashes, never breaking his gaze. "They're lovely."

"As are you." Great. Scratchy voice. Weird compliment.

Her smile grew bigger so she must have appreciated it anyway.

"Let me put these in water."

"I can do that for you," Solana offered. "Wouldn't want you to be late for your reservation."

Sydney handed the bouquet off to her roommate. "Ready?"

"Um… Yeah."

He slid his arm around her waist and led her out to the McLaren. Holding the door for her, he offered his other hand, suddenly realizing how dumb the gesture was. Like his hand would help her slide into the low-riding sports car. Dumb. Dumb. Dumb.

Once she fastened her seatbelt, he closed the door, his heart hammering against his ribs. She looked insanely gorgeous. Sexy even. A word he tried to avoid dwelling on for long. Made it too hard to keep it pure for their dating relationship if he allowed in those thoughts.

But if she were his wife? Wouldn't be off limits.

No. That would only introduce other problems. Like her eventually figuring out that he wasn't the catch she thought he was.

He sighed before he opened the door and climbed behind the wheel.

The drive to the restaurant would take almost two hours. The price of living in rural Arizona, far from the bustling Phoenix metro area.

"I'm surprised you didn't drive the Ram."

Cole reached over and squeezed her hand before releasing it to shift gears. "Seemed like a McLaren night. Happy birthday, Syd."

"Thanks."

Uh, oh. That tone. Not good.

He'd already done something wrong.

When she spoke again, the sadness or edge or whatever he'd heard was gone. Sydney filled the silence by updating him on the conversation with her parents.

"Mom wants to know if we're ever going to get married and give her grandkids."

The words sliced through him.

"I'm thirty now. As Mom so keenly pointed out, the older I am when I have kids, the more challenges there are."

Cole clamped his jaw shut so tight it twitched.

After a beat, Sydney exhaled, her shoulders slumping. "I told her to trust God's timing."

His stomach clenched even tighter. God's timing. That had been months ago. Should have been the first of Cole's pitiful failed proposal attempts. Four times he had set up memorable, special dates. She had to know at this point that he sucked at this.

Tonight. He *had* to do this tonight. No more excuses. No more fear.

SYDNEY WENT SILENT as Cole pulled onto the highway on the outskirts of Phoenix. Two-hour drive for a dinner date. Not the local Wickenburg steakhouse.

No. Not for Cole Gregory.

It would have been fine for her. She didn't care for the flashy car or truck, or threads. She'd spent years around people adorned in finery with shallow hearts. It wasn't her anymore.

The day she took the job at Vargas Sports as the Athlete Guest Services Manager had been the best day of her life. A chance to put down roots. Stop traveling the world as a tennis pro's personal assistant.

And she still got to work with her best friend Madison, who'd settled into married life surprisingly well.

That her job included working with Cole Gregory was a bonus. Or it had been.

She blinked away the sting in her eyes as she looked out the window. Streetlights popped on in the fading sunlight. In the mirror, orange and deep red splayed in glorious tones across the dusk sky.

Two years in Arizona. One year as Cole's girlfriend. Her thirtieth birthday.

The vibes he was giving off confused her. Dressed to impress. Elements at the Sanctuary? That said proposal.

Cheap flowers—so unlike him—like they were an afterthought. A pre-apology?

Sydney blinked harder, willing the tears to stay at bay.

She'd tried to stay positive. Tried to give him the space he needed to propose. He had to know she would say yes. They'd talked for almost six months about marriage. Kids. They'd prayed together and separately about it. All things pointed to a life together.

But she still had no ring on her finger.

And the conversation with Mom had put her in a poor mood. Talking about high-risk pregnancies. Pressure for grandkids, despite living halfway across the country from her parents.

Lord, please. Whatever is going on with Cole, please help him.

"Look behind us."

Sydney twisted in the leather seat. The sunset gave one final valiant burst of color before dropping behind the White Tank Mountains. It felt like a metaphor for her relationship.

"Stunning."

The silence settled again. She twisted the strap of her purse around her finger, then unwound it.

At last, Cole drove up the winding road to the mountaintop restaurant. The valet held the door open for her, practically drooling over Cole's McLaren. Sometimes she wished he'd get rid of it. Or just buy an understated SUV.

Cole offered his arm, and she looped her hand in the crook as he gave his name to the hostess. The woman led them to a secluded table lit with a cluster of three candles in the centerpiece. The view was breathtaking. Dusk silhouetted the mountain. Low-voltage landscape lighting brought the foreground of palm trees, manicured lawn, and desert scrub an angelic quality.

The perfect ambience for a birthday celebration.

Sydney wanted to hope for more, but resigned herself to less.

The server appeared with menus, explaining the evening's specials in a voice that sounded like background noise. Sydney's hands trembled slightly as she accepted hers.

"We'll start with the scallops," Cole said.

Sydney ordered water with lemon. Cole did the same.

After the server left, Cole reached across the table for her hand. His palm was warm against hers. Solid. Real.

"This place is incredible, Cole. Thank you."

"You deserve it." His voice sounded strained. "You deserve everything."

Sydney's heart stuttered. The way he was looking at her. The intensity in his eyes. This was it. This had to be it.

Say it. Please, just say it.

But the server reappeared with their waters. Cole pulled his hand back. The moment dissolved.

Sydney took a sip. The cold water did nothing to settle her stomach.

"How's the new athlete program going?" she asked, falling back on safe territory. Work. They could always talk about work. "The basketball player from Duke—did he extend his stay?"

Cole launched into details about scheduling conflicts and facility upgrades. Sydney contributed ideas about expanding the concierge services, grateful for the familiar rhythm of their conversation.

This was good. They were good together. He had to see that.

The scallops arrived perfectly seared with a delicate sauce. Sydney cut into one and nearly melted. "Oh, these are amazing. Try yours."

Cole took a bite but barely seemed to taste it. His attention kept drifting. To his pocket. To the other tables. Anywhere but her eyes.

Sydney's stomach knotted tighter.

His phone buzzed. He ignored it, which was unlike him. Cole always checked his phone.

"Are you okay?" She set down her fork. "You seem distracted."

"I'm fine. Just... thinking about how beautiful you look tonight."

The compliment should have warmed her. Instead, it felt like a deflection. He was saying what he thought she wanted to hear rather than what was really on his mind.

The server cleared their appetizer plates. Sydney's pulse quickened. Salad course next. Then entrées. How much longer would he wait?

A burst of laughter erupted from across the dining room. Sydney turned. A young couple, maybe mid-twenties. The man was on one knee. Holding up a ring box. The woman's hands covered her mouth, tears streaming.

She said yes.

The restaurant erupted in applause.

Sydney's throat tightened. That should be them. Could be them.

"That's so sweet," she whispered.

When she looked back at Cole, his jaw was clenched, face blanched. He stared at his water glass as if it held answers.

The salads arrived. Caesar for her. She picked at the romaine, her appetite gone. The earlier joy from the scallops had evaporated.

"Syd—"

"The dressing is perfect," she said quickly. Too quickly. Filling the silence before it could swallow them whole. "Exactly the right amount of lemon."

They were talking about salad dressing. On her thirtieth birthday. At a proposal-worthy restaurant.

While Cole's hands gripped his fork like he was holding on for dear life.

Lord, please. Whatever is holding him back, please help him through it. Give him courage. Give us both courage.

"Cole?" She set down her fork. "You really seem off tonight. Is something wrong?"

"Just want tonight to be perfect for you."

"It already is." The lie tasted bitter. Nothing about this felt perfect. It felt like waiting for a shoe to drop. Or a knee. Or a question that should have been asked months ago.

The server returned to clear their salad plates. "Your entrées will be out shortly. Can I get you anything else?"

Sydney shook her head. Cole said nothing.

The server left.

The silence stretched. Cole's fingers drummed against

the table. Once. Twice. Then stilled.

"The view really is stunning from up here," Sydney said, turning toward the window. Anything to break the tension. "I can see why you picked this place."

Cole didn't respond.

The entrées arrived. Waygu steak for him. Filet for her. Both looked incredible. Sydney cut hers into tiny pieces but couldn't bring herself to eat. Each bite felt like swallowing stones.

Cole forced his way through a few bites. The silence between them grew heavier. Suffocating.

This was supposed to be special. Romantic. The night everything changed.

Instead, it felt like the night everything ended.

Then Cole set down his fork. Wiped his mouth with his napkin.

Sydney's breath caught.

He pushed back his chair. Stood.

Her pulse hammered in her ears.

Cole moved around the table.

Dropped to one knee beside her chair.

Was this really happening?

The tightness in his features said no. But the knee?

He reached into his pocket and pulled out a small jewelry box. Sydney's breath caught. And held. And held. And held.

"Say something," she hissed.

He cleared his throat and stood. "Happy birthday, Syd."

Each word stabbed through her as if slowly killing everything that had been good and beautiful about their relationship. About them.

Cole opened the box to reveal…

A cross necklace. Beautiful, yes. Too expensive? Of course.

Not a ring.

His fingers fumbled as he removed it from the box and

moved behind her. Sydney's eyes burned hotter than an Arizona summer day until a tear finally spilled over. The cool metal of the cross touched her skin as she scraped her hair out of Cole's way. It took him an eternity to bring together the two ends of the chain.

Not a ring.

Be gracious.

She closed her eyes and inhaled. Then she released it softly. Slowly.

"It's. Lovely."

Cole took his seat across from her. She forced her features to relax. Or tried to.

"You like it?"

The strain in his voice was evident. She narrowed her eyes and frowned. He *had* intended to propose. And backed out. Again.

Again!

"I do."

Sydney's poor word choice split her heart wide open. This night needed to be over. Now.

"I..."

She shot to her feet. "Excuse me."

She grabbed her purse and hurried to the restroom, tears streaming down her cheeks like Vargas Wash after a monsoon. Drowning. Swallowing her heart and dreams in giant gulps.

Sydney rushed into a stall and buried her face in her hands.

Lord? What is going on? Did I hear you wrong? Do you not want us to marry? Or is it Cole? Why won't this happen?

Should I let him go?

The silence hollowed out her soul.

She didn't want to let Cole go. She wanted to be his wife. The mother of his children. She wanted to buy an overpriced house—because that's what he wanted—on the side of a mountain. Take their kids to school. Teach them about Jesus.

Grow old together.

But none of it—none of it could happen until Cole Gregory asked her.

What if he never did?

What if he enjoyed dating her but didn't know how to tell her he didn't see her as wife material? Maybe there was something wrong with her?

No. No. This had to do with something in him. Something deep. Painful.

Something he had never shared with her.

And wasn't that part of the problem?

If he couldn't trust her with his deepest secrets, then what future did they have?

Sydney dug a tissue from her purse, dabbing her eyes. They still had a two-hour drive back home. The sooner she left the sanctuary of the restroom, the sooner she could cry herself to sleep.

2

COLE COULD HARDLY breathe. The pain in Sydney's eyes gutted him. She'd read his intention—and his utter failure—for what it was.

Way to ruin her birthday.

He raised two fingers to the server. "Can you box up everything?"

"Of course."

He slid the card onto the table as his throat closed up.

The server understood the silent message. He returned quickly with their mostly uneaten meals packaged. And the receipt. Cole grossly overtipped him before stuffing his card back in his wallet. He stood carrying the bag of food, crossing to the hallway by the restrooms.

He leaned against the wall, dropping his head back. Closing his eyes, he allowed the gravity of his failure to settle into his bones.

The muffled sounds of the restaurant filtered through—laughter from a nearby table, the clink of wine glasses, someone's birthday celebration complete with off-key singing. All those people were having normal, uncomplicated evenings while he'd just destroyed the best thing in his life.

For the fifth time.

The small box in his pocket pressed against his thigh, a

physical accusation. Six months of carrying it everywhere. Six months of waiting for the perfect moment that never came. Or rather, six months of choking when the moment arrived.

Tonight was supposed to be different. Her thirtieth birthday. The milestone she'd mentioned in passing weeks ago, the biological clock comment she'd tried to make sound casual. He'd heard the hope underneath. The longing for the future she wanted. It was the same future he wanted. With her.

He'd planned everything. Made reservations at this special place. Rehearsed the words in his car. The ring had been sitting in his pocket all evening, burning a hole through the fabric.

And when the moment came—her eyes bright with anticipation—he'd frozen. Again. Watched hope flicker and die in her expression while his throat closed up and the words stayed locked inside.

Worse yet, he'd gone down on one knee. The universal signal of a proposal. Instead, he handed her the necklace.

He was going to lose her.

The women's door opened. Sydney stepped into the hallway. The bright lights behind her gave her an almost ethereal appeal.

He loved her. He. Loved. Her. And he kept hurting her anyway.

She raised her chin and straightened her shoulders as she walked past him. He fell into step behind her, placing his hand at the small of her back. Her heels clicked out a terse rhythm against the tile as she hurried outside.

Cole caught the valet's attention, and the young man darted off for his car.

"I'm sorry," he mumbled while they waited in the chilly air.

The words lit a fire, but his girlfriend—still just girlfriend—was too classy to give voice to it with an audience.

The hum of the McLaren sounded. The kid revved it a little before easing it to the curb. He tossed the keys to Cole and held the door for Sydney. Cole's jaw twitched as he rounded the car, dropping the food in the tiny space behind his seat before pulling out. He took the turns a little faster than he should have, teeth grinding.

The highway stretched ahead, headlights cutting through the darkness. Cole's mind raced, searching for something—anything—to say that would fix this. An apology that didn't sound hollow. An explanation that didn't expose his cowardice.

But every word he considered felt inadequate against the weight of what he'd done.

Sydney shifted in her seat, and he felt her gathering herself. Preparing. This wasn't over.

The air simmered as he drove. He could feel her fury in her rigid posture, her picking at her fingernails.

He'd never argued with Sydney. Not once. They'd had a few disagreements. Worked through them.

But this felt different. Like a volcano about to spew lava over their soon-to-be fossil of a relationship. There might not be any coming back from this one.

Like his clients who suffered career-ending injuries, his relationship's end seemed inevitable.

And it was all his fault.

"Do you not want me to be your wife?"

The soft words were loaded with deep hurt.

Cole cleared his throat. "I..."

She leaned forward in the low-slung passenger seat. "You don't?"

"Don't push me, Sydney."

"Push you? We first talked about marriage well over six months ago. Either you want it or you don't."

His fingers tightened on the steering wheel as his blood boiled. "Can we talk about this later?"

"Like after my ovaries shrivel up and die?!"

The words hit like a punch to the gut. Thirty. She was thirty, and he'd wasted over a year of her life. If she wanted kids—and she did, he knew she did—so did he. Every month he stalled was a month stolen from her future.

"There's no need to be crass," he said, even as shame crawled up his spine. She wasn't being crass. She was being honest. And he was still deflecting.

"When, Cole? When? When do you want to talk about whatever is eating at you?"

"Me?" He knew how wrong it was. But the truth still wouldn't come.

"Are you saying this is my fault? What is wrong with me you don't want to marry me? Are you seriously going to lead me on forever?"

The words were forming before he could stop them. Wrong words. Terrible words. The exact opposite of what she needed to hear.

"I. Need. Space."

The moment they left his mouth, he wanted to take them back. Space? She wasn't crowding him. She was asking for a future. A future they'd discussed dozens of times. But that stupid picture of Audrey and perfect Jeff was messing with his mind. He knew it, but he felt powerless to stop it.

He swallowed hard, tasting the bitterness of his own cowardice.

"Space?"

The soft-spoken question shouted louder than a stadium of roaring fans. And he was on the losing team, having fumbled the ball one too many times. He was about to get cut from the team. And all he had was a pitiful excuse.

"Are you… Do you want to break up?"

The words gutted him.

His hands went numb on the steering wheel. Break up? No. Absolutely not. Everything in him screamed against it. He wanted to marry her. Wanted to wake up next to her for the rest of his life. Wanted to give her the home and family she deserved.

But wanting wasn't enough when he couldn't make himself act.

No, he didn't want to break up. He wanted to propose. But he couldn't. Couldn't. And he couldn't get the words out of his head and through his mouth. He was that guy. Being carried out of the stadium on the cart with the towel over his head.

"No." The word finally tore from his scratchy throat. Alone. Not followed by the words he ought to say to reassure her. Not followed by "I love you" or "Please don't leave me" or "I'm sorry, I'm so sorry."

Just... no.

The silence stretched so thin Cole's nerves nearly snapped in half.

Say something. Tell her about Audrey. Tell her about the divorce you've hidden. Tell her you're terrified of failing her the way you failed your first wife. Tell her you love her more than you've ever loved anyone, and that's exactly why you're paralyzed.

But the words stayed locked behind his teeth, prisoners of his fear.

This was on him. It was up to him to fix it.

And if it were anything else, he would. He could. But this felt insurmountable.

Then, the soft sobs started as the lights of Wickenburg came into view.

Each broken breath from the passenger seat was a knife to his chest. He'd done this. Reduced this strong, capable woman to tears on her birthday. The same woman who'd reorganized his entire life, who'd made him want to be better, who'd brought joy back into his carefully controlled existence.

Leaving her disappointed. Confused. Gave her a beautiful necklace that meant *not yet* when she needed *forever*.

Cole pursed his lips, fighting against the burn in his own eyes.

His arm ached with the need to touch her. Hold her hand. Something. But he gripped the wheel tighter. Turned onto the gravel drive. Parked in front of her home.

She flung the door open without waiting for him.

Fine. Just fine.

Then his heart ran inside her home, slamming the door shut.

On him. On his failure.

Cole jammed the shifter in reverse, kicking up a spray of gravel as he backed out. Then he jammed it into drive, laying hard on the accelerator, fishtailing as he rounded the end of the dirt road.

When he finally parked in front of his rental, he sat there. Unmoving. The food aroma turned his stomach.

She forgot her meal.

He let out a humorless laugh. Of all the stupid thoughts he could have.

The ring box pressed against his thigh.

Six months ago, he hadn't hesitated.

It had started at the double-wide. Derin and Madison's place while their house was still being framed out, back when the four of them had fallen into a loose rhythm of Sunday dinners and easy evenings. Cole had lived in that double-wide with Derin before he married. He knew every creak in the floor, every cabinet that stuck, every light that took two tries.

But that night, Sydney was in the kitchen.

She and Madison were making butter chicken, some recipe Sydney had pulled from a dog-eared card she'd brought from Iowa. The whole place smelled like warm spice and garlic, and Sydney had tied on one of Madison's aprons—ruffled, ridiculous, bright yellow. A dusting of something on her cheek, and she didn't know it. She was laughing at something Madison said, her whole face unguarded as if she felt completely at home.

Cole had leaned against the doorframe and watched.

Then she looked up.

Just for a second. Green eyes finding his across the small kitchen, warm and easy, like he was exactly where he was supposed to be.

That was it. That was the whole thing.

He wanted her in his kitchen. In his life. Waking up in his house, wearing a ridiculous apron, with something on her cheek she didn't know about. He wanted to be the one who told her. He wanted to be the one she laughed with at the end of the day, every day, for the rest of his life.

No second-guessing. No fine print. Just Sydney.

He'd driven into Wickenburg the next morning. Nothing there was right. So he got on the highway and drove to Scottsdale, two hours away, and walked into the first jewelry store with intention in his step. Wrong store. Second store, same story. Third store, close but not quite.

Fourth store.

Round stone. White gold setting. Small diamonds trailing down each side. Simple. Classic. Exactly her.

Him and her, in jewelry form.

He'd bought it before doubt could talk him out of it. Driven home with the little velvet box on the passenger seat. The whole way back, he'd imagined her face when she saw it.

Then the first Instagram notification had come in. Audrey. Her perfect new kitchen. Her perfect new husband. Her perfect new life, the one that looked nothing like what they'd had together.

He'd told himself it didn't matter. Told himself that was then and this was now.

But the doubt had moved in anyway, quiet and patient. Not about Sydney. Never about Sydney. About him. About whether a man who'd failed once was fool enough to believe he wouldn't fail again. Whether he'd wake up one day and find he'd turned into the same version of himself that had chosen ambition over a marriage.

The ring had moved from pocket to pocket for six months while he waited to feel sure enough.

He still wasn't sure.

Cole climbed out of the McLaren. The porch light flickered on. He stood there in the dark with a bag of cold food and a ring he still couldn't bring himself to offer, staring at a house he'd never bothered to make into a home.

The man who'd driven two hours to find the right ring.

Same man who'd just handed her a necklace instead.

Inside, he dropped the bag on the kitchen counter. Pulled out the containers and stared at them. Seventy-dollar steaks, barely touched. Sides still warm. Her favorite dessert waiting in its little box.

All wasted.

Like everything else tonight.

His hand went to his pocket. The small box sat there. He pulled it out and flipped open the ring box. The diamond caught the overhead light, throwing tiny rainbows across the granite countertop. Beautiful. Perfect. Just like her.

And he still couldn't do it.

Cole snapped the box shut. Shoved it back in his pocket. The ring had burned a hole through five different pockets over six months. Number five. The fifth time he'd almost done it. Five times he'd choked.

And he'd lashed out at her. At Sydney. The woman he'd loved deeper than he ever had Audrey. Sydney who deserved a permanent home. Kids. A husband who had her back.

A man who could actually ask her to be his wife.

After tonight, Cole wasn't even sure she'd take his calls.

SYDNEY STORMED INSIDE, grabbed the vase of cheap flowers and dumped them into the trash can, ignoring her roommates' greetings. Then she fled to her room, flopping face-first onto her bed. Her heels slipped off her feet, landing on the carpet with a muted thud.

Like the numb thud of her heart.

After a moment, she pushed up and caught sight of herself in the mirror above her dresser.

The green dress that had taken her an hour to choose. Not too formal, not too casual. The perfect shade to complement her coloring. She'd curled her hair, done her makeup carefully. Even splurged on new heels.

And the greeting. Heat flushed her cheeks, remembering how she'd kissed him on the lips instead of their usual chaste peck on the cheek. A small signal—*I'm ready. Tonight, I'm ready to answer "yes."*

She'd tried to make it easy for him. Created the perfect moment. Looked her best. Shown him she wanted a lifetime together.

Maybe mentioning her mom's comment about grandkids had been a mistake. That alone couldn't have created this much pressure, could it?

Sydney's reflection stared back at her—mascara smudged, eyes red and swollen, the beautiful dress now wrinkled from lying on the bed.

All that effort. All that hope.

For a necklace.

Five times. He almost proposed five times.

And he had nothing to say to her direct question.

She grabbed the pillow and hugged it close to her chest.

Where did this leave them? Or was there even a "them" anymore?

A soft knock sounded on her door. "Syd?"

Solana.

Sydney pressed her face into the pillow to stifle her sobs.

The door creaked open. Footsteps padded across the carpet. The bed dipped as someone sat beside her.

"Oh, honey." Renata's hand settled on her back, rubbing gentle circles.

Sydney's shoulders shook with fresh sobs. She couldn't hold it together. Not tonight.

"What happened?" Solana's voice came from her other side.

Sydney dropped the pillow into her lap. Her eyelids felt puffy and swollen. Her pale skin probably looked as blotchy as she felt. Both women sat on her bed, concern etched across their faces. The beautiful green dress felt like a costume now. A joke.

"He..." Sydney's voice cracked. She touched the cross at her throat. "He gave me this."

Renata's gaze dropped to the necklace. Understanding flooded her features.

"It's beautiful," Solana said carefully.

"It is." Sydney's fingers traced the delicate metalwork. White gold. Probably custom. Exactly the kind of thoughtful, classy gift Cole would choose. The cross itself was simple but elegant. Something she'd treasure forever.

"But it's not a ring."

"No, it's not," Renata whispered.

Sydney shook her head, fresh tears spilling. "He got down on one knee. At the restaurant. In front of everyone. I thought... I really thought..."

Solana sucked in a sharp breath.

"Then he just... stood up. Gave me the necklace. Happy birthday." Sydney laughed, but it came out bitter. Wrong. "He dropped to one knee and gave me a necklace."

"Oh, Syd." Renata pulled her into a hug.

"This was the fifth time." The words tumbled out, hot and fast. "Christmas. Valentine's Day. That trail ride was last month. A random Tuesday at work. And tonight. Five times I could feel him working up to it. Five times he backed out."

"You've been counting." Solana's tone held no judgment. Just sadness.

"How could I not?" Sydney pulled back, swiping at her cheeks. "The first time I thought maybe I was imagining things. By the third time, I knew. And tonight..." She touched the cross again. "I asked him point-blank."

Renata winced. "What did he say?"

"That I was pushing him. That he needed space." Sydney's voice dropped to a whisper. "I asked if he wanted to break up. He said no, but Renata, what else am I supposed to think?"

The silence stretched between them.

"What are you going to do?" Solana finally asked.

Sydney looked around her room. The first real home she'd had in years. Photos on the wall from Bible study nights. Her worn Bible on the nightstand, with passages underlined and notes scribbled in the margins.

This place. These women. The Vargas family and their fierce, faithful love. The community she'd found here.

She'd built a life at this ranch. Put down roots for the first time in her adult existence.

But she couldn't keep doing this. Couldn't keep waiting. Living in limbo. Working with Cole every day while he refused to choose her. Not fully. Not permanently.

"I don't know." Sydney's throat tightened. "I can't keep living like this. But I don't know what to do about it."

Renata squeezed her hand. Solana brushed a strand of hair from Sydney's face.

They stayed like that for a long time. Sydney between her two friends, their quiet presence saying more than words could.

Eventually, they said goodnight. Reminded her they were just down the hall if she needed anything. Left her alone with her thoughts and her beautiful, perfectly chosen, utterly wrong birthday gift.

Sydney changed into pajamas and climbed under the covers. Her fingers found the cross again in the darkness.

Lord, I don't understand. I thought this was Your plan. Thought Cole was the one. But if he can't even propose after one year, after talking about marriage for six months... what am I sup-

posed to do?

She waited for an answer. For peace. For anything.

But the only sound was her own heartbeat and the muffled voices of her roommates in the living room, probably praying for her.

Sydney closed her eyes.

Maybe some prayers didn't get answered the way she'd hoped.

Sydney sat up in the darkness and reached behind her neck. The clasp of the necklace gave easily, and she pulled it off, holding it in her palm.

The bathroom nightlight cast just enough glow for her to see the delicate metalwork. She crossed to her dresser and laid the necklace carefully on the smooth surface.

That's when she noticed them.

Tiny roses. A vine of them growing around the cross, so intricate she'd missed them in the dim restaurant lighting and her emotional fog. Each petal perfectly formed. Each thorn visible.

Her throat tightened.

It was an expression of his love. Custom-made. Thoughtful. Beautiful.

That was part of the problem, wasn't it? She knew Cole loved her. Knew he wanted to marry her. His actions showed it every day—the way he looked at her, the way he prioritized time with her, the careful attention he paid to things she mentioned in passing.

But she was completely dumbfounded by the numerous failed proposals. Lack of confidence was so far from the man she knew and loved. Cole Gregory didn't hesitate. He was decisive. Commanded rooms full of professional athletes. Negotiated million-dollar contracts.

This truly was something going on in his heart, and she didn't know how to help him.

Couldn't help someone who wouldn't let her in.

Sydney climbed back into bed, pulling the covers up to

her chin. The necklace gleamed softly in the darkness, beautiful and wrong, a symbol of everything they were—and everything they couldn't seem to become.

And tomorrow—ugh, Thursday—she would put it on again, praying that it would send the right signal to Cole. She still loved him. Was still ready for their future together.

For now.

3

COLE PULLED INTO the Vargas Sports parking lot at five-thirty in the morning, headlights cutting through the pre-dawn darkness. The McLaren's engine purred to silence as he killed the ignition, and the quiet settled over him.

He should go inside. Get to work. Pretend last night hadn't happened.

But his hands stayed locked on the steering wheel, knuckles white in the dim glow of the dashboard lights.

Sydney's face. The way her smile had frozen when he opened that jewelry box. The flicker of hope in her eyes died as she realized what *wasn't* there.

He'd seen it. Every second of it. And he'd sat there like a coward, unable to fix what he'd broken.

Cole forced himself out of the car and locked it, the beep echoing across the empty lot. His dress shoes clicked against the pavement as he headed for the entrance. The building loomed in the dark. He had at least two hours before anyone else showed up. Two hours to pull himself together before he had to face Sydney across a conference table, or in the hallway, or anywhere that required him to act normal.

Normal. As if anything about this was normal.

Inside, he flipped the lights on as he went; the familiar route to his office grounding him. Computer on. Coffee started. Email open. The motions of a regular Thursday morning.

Except nothing about this morning was regular.

He sank into his desk chair and stared at the dark screen as the computer booted up. The office felt too quiet. Too empty. Or maybe he just felt too empty, and the office was only reflecting what was already inside him.

Last night replayed on a loop. The restaurant. The candlelight. The perfect gift. A white-gold cross necklace with a vine of roses, delicate and beautiful. Meaningful. A gift that said he knew her, he saw her faith, and he cared about what mattered to her.

Just not the gift she'd wanted.

Not the gift she deserved.

His phone sat on the desk beside his keyboard, screen dark and silent. No messages. Nothing from Sydney since she'd stormed out of the McLaren last night without a word.

Cole pulled up his calendar. Back-to-back meetings today. Operations review at nine. Staff check-in at ten-thirty. Athlete program coordination at one. All of it required him to be present and focused. Pretend he wasn't falling apart.

The coffee maker beeped. He pushed back from his desk and went to pour a cup, black and strong. The first sip burned, but he welcomed it. Something to feel besides the hollow ache in his chest.

He'd wanted to propose. Had the ring in his pocket the entire dinner. Had rehearsed the words a hundred times.

Simple. Honest. True.

But when the moment came, when she had looked at him with those green eyes full of hope and trust, fear had grabbed him by the throat and refused to let go.

Same fear as before. Same failure.

Cole set the coffee mug down harder than he meant to; the sharp crack of ceramic against wood startling in the silence. He braced his hands on the counter and let his head drop forward.

He had to stop this. Had to get his head together before

people started arriving. Before he had to face Derin's knowing looks or Madison's worried questions, or worse, Sydney's carefully blank professionalism.

His phone chimed with an incoming email. He ignored it and grabbed his coffee, heading back to his desk. Work. He could lose himself in work. Answer emails, review schedules, and handle the dozen small fires that always needed attention.

Anything to stop thinking about the way hope had died in her eyes.

The memory hit him without warning.

Not last night. Further back. Fifteen, sixteen months ago. January. A few days after Madison Moore had arrived.

Derin had put his foot in his mouth on the tennis court, and Cole had spent the better part of an hour at Madison's casita talking her and her manager down from canceling the reservation entirely. It hadn't been his finest afternoon. Her manager had been immovable. Madison had been furious. And Cole had done a lot of listening before either of them started to thaw.

But Sydney had been there.

Most people looked right past her. Cole had watched it happen a dozen times that first week. Guests would approach Madison's group, eyes drawn to the tennis star like moths to a flame, barely registering the petite redhead with the freckled cheeks and careful smile.

But Cole had noticed her.

It had started with a simple question. Madison and her manager had been deep in a debate about whether to leave, and Cole had stepped back and turned to Sydney with an apologetic grin. "Are they always like this?"

She'd smiled. Small at first, then wider, her entire face transformed with warmth and humor. "Only when they're being stubborn. So yes, often."

One conversation. Ten minutes, maybe. But in those ten minutes, he'd learned she was Madison's personal assistant.

That she'd been working in professional tennis for three years. That she was tired of traveling and wanted to put down roots somewhere. That she loved old movies and terrible puns and had a laugh that made him want to keep talking just to hear it again.

One conversation, and he'd known she was someone special.

Someone worth knowing.

Someone worth loving.

The memory settled over him, bittersweet and sharp. He'd known it then.

And now he was the one who couldn't give her what she wanted.

Couldn't give her the commitment she deserved.

Couldn't give her the future she'd been brave enough to dream about while he stood paralyzed by fear.

Cole opened his email and started working through messages, forcing his mind to focus on anything but the weight of his own failure.

The sun had risen when he heard voices in the hallway. He glanced at the clock. Seven-thirty. Right on schedule.

Footsteps approached his office, and he braced himself. Probably Ryan or Hudson, ready to discuss the day's training sessions.

But it was Madison who appeared in his doorway, and one look at her face told him everything he needed to know. She was furious.

"My best friend," Madison said, voice tight with barely controlled anger, "did not text me with good news last night."

Her heels clicked against the tile floor as she stepped closer.

"Just a picture of her empty hand."

Cole's stomach dropped.

"Madi." Derin's voice came from behind her, gentle but firm. "Let me handle this."

"Handle what?" Madison spun to face her husband. "He had the perfect opportunity. Her birthday. And he—"

"Madi." Derin caught her hand, his expression understanding but resolute. "Come on."

"But—"

"I know." Derin squeezed her hand. "But this is between Cole and Sydney. And right now, between Cole and me."

Madison's lips pressed into a thin line, but she let Derin guide her away from the door. Cole heard their footsteps retreat down the hall, heard the low murmur of Derin's voice and Madison's sharp response.

Then Derin was back, closing the office door behind him.

He didn't sit. Just stood there, studying Cole with a look that didn't need words.

"Bro." Quiet. Direct. "What happened?"

Cole opened his mouth. Closed it. "I choked. Had the moment, had the plan, and just couldn't."

"The ring?"

"In my pocket the entire night."

Derin shook his head slowly before crossing his arms. "So what's the holdup?"

Cole stared at his coffee. "I don't know."

A beat of silence. Derin let it sit there, which was somehow harder than if he'd pushed.

"You know you can talk to me," Derin said finally. "Whatever it is."

Cole knew Derin would listen. Of all people, he'd probably understand. But the secret had weighed on him for so long.

"I know," Cole said. "I just need to work through it."

Derin studied him a moment longer. "Don't let it go too long."

Then he was gone, and Cole was alone again with his coffee and his cowardice.

Derin was right. He knew that. But knowing it and doing something about it were two different things.

Cole pulled up his phone and opened his contacts. The florist he'd used before. They'd delivered to Sydney at her office last time, a congratulations arrangement when she'd closed a big deal with a new athlete association.

This time, he needed something different.

His fingers moved across the screen, typing out the order. A dozen roses. Pink, Sydney's favorite. Delivered to her office at Vargas Sports.

Card message: *I'm sorry.*

The same message he'd sent Audrey years ago, after one of their fights. After he'd chosen a client meeting over their anniversary dinner. After he'd missed her birthday because of a contract negotiation that couldn't wait.

"I'm sorry" had never been enough then.

But it was all he knew how to say now.

He confirmed the order and set his phone down. The flowers would arrive mid-morning. Sydney would get them. Maybe they'd help. Show her he knew he'd messed up. Buy him enough time to figure out what to do next.

Maybe.

Cole threw himself into work, answering emails and reviewing schedules. When Ryan knocked on his door at eight-thirty to discuss a new physical therapy protocol, Cole was grateful for the distraction.

But the whole time, part of his mind stayed fixed on the clock. Watching. Waiting.

The flowers arrived at nine-forty-five.

Cole heard the delivery person in the lobby, heard the cheerful exchange with the receptionist. His office door was open a crack, and he peered through it down the hallway.

The receptionist walked toward Sydney's office, a vase of pink roses in hand.

Cole's heart hammered against his ribs.

He shouldn't be watching this. It was an invasion of privacy. Pathetic.

But he couldn't look away.

Sydney's door was open. He could just see her at her desk, head bent over her computer. The receptionist knocked lightly on the doorframe, and Sydney looked up.

Her expression shifted when she saw the flowers. A frown.

Then she took the card.

Cole watched her read it. Watched her face.

And saw the exact moment his apology landed.

No smile. No softening. Just a flicker of something that looked like pain, quickly shuttered behind careful blankness.

She thanked the receptionist. Set the flowers on the corner of her desk. Turned back to her computer.

As if nothing had happened.

Like the roses meant nothing.

Cole stepped back from the door. The air went out of him. The flowers hadn't helped. If anything, they'd made it worse.

Because Sydney didn't want his apologies.

She wanted his commitment.

And he couldn't give her that. Not without the truth. Not without confessing everything he'd spent years hiding.

Not without risking her looking at him the way she'd just looked at those roses.

Like a beautiful gesture that meant nothing at all.

A clearing throat drew his attention. Heat warmed his face and neck as he stepped back, holding the door open for the Quaids.

He'd forgotten they were on his calendar.

Parker Quaid took the seat across from Cole's desk, hat in his lap, at ease the way men who worked outdoors tended to be. His wife sat beside him, tablet open, a printed proposal on the edge of Cole's desk between them.

Shannon Quaid ran Braden's Hope with a precision that made Cole's job easier every time their departments intersected. She'd built the equine therapy program from almost nothing over the last year. Parker's role was quieter—warming up the horses before sessions, cooling them down after, the steady behind-the-scenes work that kept Shannon's vision running.

"We'd like to expand athlete involvement in two ways," Shannon said. "First, some of your rehab athletes could participate in the equine therapy themselves. Time with horses has a measurable impact on mental recovery. Second, we'd love to offer athletes the chance to volunteer with our clients—the disabled kids and veterans in the program. Both options would be completely voluntary, worked around your PT team's schedule."

Cole picked up the proposal and scanned the first page. Clean formatting. Solid data. "How many hours per week?"

"Two to start. We scale based on interest and your team's sign-off."

Parker leaned forward. "You've seen it yourself, Cole. What the joy on those kids' faces can do for a hurting soul. Would give the athletes something to look forward to that has nothing to do with their own troubles."

Shannon's eyes cut to her husband. Quick, warm, unguarded.

Something tightened in Cole's gut.

He'd seen that ease between them before, at church, around the ranch. They hadn't dated long before Parker proposed. A few months, if Cole remembered right. He had paid little attention at the time.

He was paying attention now.

"Marco Rossi has been asking about the horses," Cole said, pulling his focus back to the page. "I'll have Madison review the scheduling piece and get back to you by the end of the week."

"That works." Shannon closed her tablet. "Parker can work with Marco directly."

They stood, and Cole walked them to the door. Parker held it open for Shannon, one hand resting at the small of her back. She said something low, just for him, and he laughed as they turned down the hallway.

The door swung shut.

Cole stood at his desk for a moment, the proposal in his hand, not reading it.

A few months. That was apparently all some people needed.

He set the proposal on the stack he wouldn't touch until tomorrow and went back to work.

His phone buzzed. A text.

Sydney: *Can I stop by your place after work?*

Cole stared at the screen. Hours from now, she'd be at his house. In the space he'd never fully unpacked. In the life he'd never fully committed to.

And he'd have to face her knowing that flowers and apologies weren't enough.

Knowing that nothing he could offer would ever be enough.

Not without the truth.

And the truth was the one thing he couldn't give.

Cole: *Of course. I'll be there by 6.*

He hit send and set the phone down.

Six o'clock. He had until six o'clock to figure out what to say to the woman he loved.

The woman he was losing.

The woman who deserved so much better than a man who couldn't even be honest about his past.

SYDNEY PULLED INTO her usual parking spot at Vargas Sports just after seven. Cole's McLaren sat in his reserved space near the entrance. The ridiculous lime-green paint was impossible to miss even in the early morning light.

So he'd come in early. Avoiding her, probably.

She grabbed her bag and headed inside, keeping her

eyes on the glass doors ahead instead of glancing toward his office windows. The building felt quiet, empty except for the low hum of the HVAC system and the distant sound of someone's radio playing classic country.

His office lights were on. She could see the warm glow spilling into the hallway as she approached.

Every other morning for more than a year, she would have turned left. Walked down that hallway. Knocked on his doorframe even though it was always open. Said good morning. Poured herself coffee from the pot he always started before she arrived. Sat in the chair across from his desk while they sipped and talked through the day ahead.

Praying together for their clients. For their friends. For each other.

It had become the best part of her morning. The quiet rhythm of starting each day together.

Today, she turned right. Straight to her own office. Closed the door. Set her bag on the desk and sank into her chair.

Her fingers found the necklace at her throat. White gold, delicate, the tiny vine of roses winding around the cross, the texture smooth against her fingertips. She'd put it on this morning hoping he'd see it. Hoping he'd understand that storming out of his car last night wasn't outright rejection.

Just pain.

Just the weight of another milestone birthday without the future she'd been waiting for.

Sydney powered on her computer and forced herself to focus on her calendar. Thursday. Full day. Meeting with Chef at ten about Carter Wakefield's dietary requirements. Check-in with Renata about his casita. Probably a dozen small fires to put out between now and five o'clock.

And then tonight. Cole's house. The conversation they both knew had to come.

Her stomach twisted.

She pulled up Carter's file and started making notes.

MLB pitcher, shoulder injury, six-week rehab stay. High-fiber carbs, no processed sugars, and high-protein to maintain muscle mass during recovery. She'd coordinate with Chef to make sure they had everything lined up before Carter arrived this afternoon.

Work. She could lose herself in work.

A knock on her doorframe made her look up.

The receptionist stood there with a vase of pink roses, a small white card tucked among the blooms.

Sydney's heart stuttered.

"Delivery for you," the receptionist said with a bright smile. "Someone's got an admirer."

Sydney managed a smile she didn't feel and thanked her, waiting until the woman left before reaching for the card.

Two words: *I'm sorry. C.*

She set the card down carefully. Stared at the roses. Pink. Her favorite. He'd remembered.

But flowers didn't answer the question she couldn't stop asking herself. If he wanted to marry her, why hadn't he? He'd said the words. He'd let her believe it. She'd seen the way he looked at her and thought she understood what it meant.

Except the moment had come and gone. She had no ring on her finger to prove his love. Instead, all she had was a card the size of her palm and a dozen roses she didn't want.

She'd been patient. She'd given him time. She'd told herself that love didn't run on a schedule, even while her thirtieth birthday had come and gone, the future she wanted slipping through her fingers.

But he'd said he wanted to marry her. For months they'd discussed it. And she'd held onto his words like they were a promise.

Maybe that was the problem. She'd been holding onto words when she needed more than that.

Sydney moved the vase to the corner of her desk and

turned back to her computer.

Work. Just focus on work.

A few minutes before ten, she stood and headed toward the dining hall for her meeting with Chef. The surly cowboy chef had taken some getting used to when she first started, until she learned that beneath his gruff exterior was a teddy bear. Most people didn't spend enough time with him to see it though.

"Morning," she said, hovering near the entrance of the kitchen. "Got a few minutes to talk about our new client?"

Chef looked up with a nod. "The pitcher. Carter Wakefield, right?"

Sydney pulled up her notes on her tablet and relayed his dietary requirements. "He's coming off shoulder surgery, so he'll be working hard in PT. Needs to maintain muscle mass without compromising the healing process."

Chef made notes on his tablet. "I can do high-fiber carb bowls, quinoa combinations, grilled chicken and fish for protein. Does he like spicy?"

"I'll check and let you know." Sydney added it to her list. "He's also bringing his daughter with him off and on during the stay. She's five."

"Noted." Chef looked up. "When does he arrive?"

"This afternoon around three. I'll send you his full file before then."

"Perfect." Chef set his tablet down. "How are you doing?"

The question caught her off guard. Chef wasn't usually one for small talk.

"Fine," she said automatically. "Just busy."

Chef's expression said he didn't believe her, but he didn't push.

Sydney left before the concern in his eyes could undo the careful composure she had maintained all morning.

Renata's office was her next stop. Her roommate looked up from her computer with a warm smile.

"Sydney! What can I do for you?"

"Carter Wakefield. Checking on his casita for this afternoon."

"All set." Renata pulled up her screen. "Cholla Casita. It's a one-bedroom one. I heard he might have his daughter with him?"

"Off and on during his stay. Is the pull-out sofa bed in good shape?"

"Just replaced the mattress last month. Should be comfortable for her." Renata made a note. "Anything else he needs?"

"Not that I can think of. I'll let you know if something comes up."

Sydney left the resort office and started back toward the sports complex, her path taking her along the walking trail that wound through the property. The sun warmed her shoulders, and the familiar desert landscape spread out around her.

She slowed her pace, letting the quiet settle over her.

What's wrong with me?

The question had been circling in her mind since last night. Since the moment she'd seen that jewelry box, and felt hope rise, then crash.

What am I doing wrong? Why isn't he ready? What more can I do to prove I'm worth committing to?

Sydney stopped walking. Closed her eyes.

No.

She knew better than this. She'd spent the past three years learning to control her thoughts, to recognize the lies and replace them with truth.

This wasn't about her worth.

This was about whatever Cole carried and wouldn't share.

Lord, I don't know what's wrong. I don't know why he won't talk to me. And I'm scared. I'm scared this is it. That tonight is the end.

A light breeze stirred the desert brush around her.

Give me wisdom. Help me know what to say. How to listen. Whether to stay or whether to walk away. Show me what You would have me learn through this.

The prayer didn't make the knot in her stomach disappear, but it shifted something. Loosened the grip of fear just enough to let her breathe.

Sydney opened her eyes and continued toward the sports complex.

Tonight. Whatever happened, she'd face it. With or without Cole.

At three o'clock, Sydney waited in the resort office as a blue Ford F-150 parked near the entrance. Carter Wakefield climbed out, favoring his right shoulder.

She stepped outside with a professional smile. "Carter? I'm Sydney Steele, your athlete services coordinator. Welcome to Vargas Ranch."

"Thanks." He shook her hand with his left, his awkward grip firm despite the injury. Late twenties, tall, with the lean build of a pitcher. His right arm hung in a sling. "Appreciate you folks taking me on short notice."

"Not a problem. We're glad to have you." Sydney gestured toward the entrance. "Let me show you to your casita, and then we can go over your schedule."

She led him along the path to the Cholla Casita, explaining the layout of the property as they walked. Carter asked questions about his recovery plan.

"Your first PT session is scheduled for tomorrow morning at eight with Ryan," Sydney said as she unlocked the casita door. "And I've coordinated with our chef about your dietary needs. If anything doesn't work or you need adjustments, just let me know."

Carter stepped inside and set his bag down, looking around the space with approval. "This is perfect. Better than most hotels I've stayed in."

"The bedroom is through there." Sydney pointed. "I

understand your daughter might be joining you?"

"Yeah." His expression softened. "Reed's coming Saturday. She'll stay for a week, then head back home."

"She's five, right?"

"Just. And full of energy." He smiled. "Hope that's okay."

"Absolutely. The casita has a pull-out sofa bed. Let me know if I can do anything to make her stay comfortable." Sydney flipped open her tablet. "Does she have any dietary restrictions we should know about?"

"Nope. She'll eat just about anything." He paused. "This is really above and beyond. Thank you."

"It's what we do." Sydney handed him a folder. "Here's your welcome packet with the schedule, facility information, and my contact details. I'm your primary contact for anything you need during your stay."

Carter flipped through the folder. "Cole mentioned you were good at this."

Sydney's heart skipped a beat. "You know Cole?"

"He was my agent before he left to come work here. He reached out when he heard about my injury, told me about this place." Carter looked up. "Said you'd take good care of me."

"We will." Sydney kept her voice steady despite the tightness in her throat. "He's done a fantastic job creating the programs for football and baseball players."

"No surprise there. He was an amazing agent. Really got to know me on a personal level."

"I noticed on your profile, you mentioned Christian as your religious preference."

Carter's eyes brightened. "Yeah. Cole actually led me to Christ."

Her heart softened a little. It was one thing she loved most about her boyfriend. Always bringing hope to athletes. Pointing them toward Jesus.

"We have space in the Tuesday and Thursday Men's Bible Study. If you're interested, just email or text me and I'll reserve a spot for you."

"Yeah, that'd be great. Go ahead and put me down. And if you have any info about activities for Reed during the day, could you send me that?"

"Absolutely." She let out a soft laugh. "I should let you get settled now. If you need anything, just call or text. Otherwise, I'll see you tomorrow morning to walk you over to PT."

"Sounds good."

Sydney left the casita and walked back towards the sports complex. The afternoon sun beat down on the path.

Cole had led Carter to Christ. That was the Cole she knew. The man who cared deeply about people, who invested in their lives beyond the surface level. The man who'd built programs that didn't just rehabilitate bodies but restored hope.

The man who couldn't seem to commit to a future with her.

The dichotomy was hard to reconcile.

What had happened in Cole's life? Something must have caused him to choke with proposing. And why wouldn't he tell her about it?

Back at her office, Sydney sent Carter the additional information and worked through the rest of her afternoon tasks. Emails. Started planning for another new client. She pushed the thoughts away, determined to focus on work for the rest of the day.

At the end of her day, she shut down her computer and grabbed her bag before heading over to the dining hall.

"Hey, Syd." The hostess greeted her. "What can I get you?"

"Two to-go containers. Chicken Caesar for me. Meatloaf and the house salad for Cole."

Cole's favorite. The kitchen staff made it every Thursday, and he always ordered it when they ate on property.

The woman packed up the containers and handed them over with a smile. Sydney thanked her and headed out to her car.

The drive to Forepaugh took only a few minutes, ranch property giving way to the small cluster of houses that made up the town. Cole's rental was on the east side, a modest single-story with a two-car garage and a perfectly manicured lawn. Not a blade of grass out of place or overgrown.

Sydney pulled into the driveway behind the McLaren and sat for a moment, staring at the house.

It had been months since she'd been here. They spent so much time on ranch property or at Derin and Madison's place, or in town that coming to Cole's rental had become a rarity. She'd almost forgotten what it looked like.

She grabbed the food containers and her bag and walked to the front door. Knocked.

Cole answered within seconds, as if he'd been waiting, still dressed in his expensive work clothes. Though he'd rolled up the sleeves on his button-down shirt.

"Hey."

"Hey." Sydney held up the containers. "Brought dinner."

His expression softened. "You didn't have to do that."

"I know."

He stepped back to let her in, and Sydney walked into the living room.

And stopped.

Cardboard boxes. Everywhere. Stacked against the walls, lining the hallway, filling the corners. Some labeled with black marker, most not. The couch looked lived-in, and the TV was set up, but everything else screamed temporary.

Like he'd moved in yesterday instead of ten months ago, right before Derin and Madison's wedding.

Sydney set the food containers on the kitchen counter, her mind racing.

The unpacked boxes. The rental instead of buying. The

McLaren he refused to trade for something practical.

All of it. Everything she'd been trying to ignore suddenly came into focus.

"Cole." Sydney's pulse slowed, a chill washing over her. "How long have you lived here?"

He stood between the living room and the kitchen, hands in his pockets. "You know how long."

"Ten months." She turned to look at him. "You've lived here for ten months, and you haven't unpacked?"

4

HEAT FLOODED COLE'S face, creeping up his neck and settling in the tips of his ears. The truth sat in cardboard boxes all around them, stacked against walls, lining the hallway, filling corners. Ten months. He'd lived here ten months and hadn't unpacked.

"I just... haven't gotten around to it." The words came out mumbled, pathetic even to his own ears.

Sydney stood in the middle of his living room, those emerald eyes cataloging every taped box, every temporary surface, every piece of evidence that he'd never committed to this life. To this town. To her.

He couldn't let her stand there staring at his failures. "Let's eat." Cole gestured toward the kitchen counter where she'd set the to-go containers. "Before it gets cold."

She followed him without a word, her footsteps soft on the hardwood floor he'd never bothered to cover with rugs. He grabbed two plates from the cupboard and divided the food. Meatloaf and house salad for him. Chicken Caesar for her.

Honestly, he kinda deserved her ire. And was a little surprised she hadn't caught him sooner. They'd agreed that it wasn't a good idea to spend too much time alone at his place while dating. Too much temptation to cross lines they both wanted to save for marriage.

Except she didn't know—didn't know he'd already been married once before.

His stomach sank as he led her to the small dining table. The movers had dropped it in place the day he moved. Same with the couch, bed, and dresser. Everything else remained in boxes except for one box of kitchen items and some boxes of clothes.

Cole bowed his head, aware of Sydney's eyes still on him. "Father, thank You for this food and for Sydney bringing it. Thank You for Your provision and Your presence with us. Guide our conversation tonight. Give us wisdom and grace. In Jesus' name, amen."

"Amen," Sydney murmured.

Cole lifted his fork. The meatloaf smelled amazing but turned to sawdust in his dry mouth. Across from him, Sydney stabbed at her Caesar salad with sharp, precise movements. Fork hitting lettuce. Fork scraping plate. The sound grated against the silence, chipping away at his composure.

Another failure on his part. The dinner. The evening. All of it.

He took another bite. Chewed mechanically. Swallowed. The clock on the wall ticked loudly. Sydney's fork clinked against ceramic. He could feel her tension radiating across the small table.

Say something. Anything.

But what? The boxes spoke for themselves. The McLaren in the driveway. The rental agreement instead of a mortgage. Everything about his life here screamed temporary.

The silence wrapped around his throat.

"I thought you wanted to put down roots." Sydney's voice cut through the quiet, controlled but tight.

Cole looked up from his plate and held her gaze. "I do."

"Just look around." She set her fork down carefully, deliberately. Her hand trembled slightly. "You know what I see? I see a man who hasn't unpacked his belongings in ten months. Ten. A man who says he wants a stable life. A quieter life. But still drives around in an extremely overpriced sports car for the area we live in."

"I have a truck." The words came out sharply.

"A Ram TRX that costs more than most people's annual salary. That's not the point."

"Then what is the point?" He pushed back from the table slightly.

Sydney's eyes met his, unflinching. "The heart is more deceitful than anything else, and incurable—who can understand it? Jeremiah 17:9."

The verse hit like a punch to the gut. Cole's jaw clenched. "So you're saying I'm lying to you?"

"I'm saying maybe you're lying to yourself." Her voice softened, but the words still cut deep. "Do you really want this life? Your job here at the ranch? Or are you just biding time until you can go back to being a sports agent?"

"No." The response came quickly. "I love my job. I love working with the athletes, building the programs, helping guys like Carter—"

"Then why won't you settle in?" Sydney gestured around the room, taking in the boxes, the bare walls, the lack of anything personal or permanent. "Why do you live as if you're ready to leave at any moment? You've been here long enough to know whether or not this is your home."

Cole's throat constricted. Because home meant permanence. Permanent meant commitment. Commitment meant risk.

And risk meant the possibility of failing again.

"I am settled." Even as he said it, he knew how false it sounded.

"Really?" Sydney picked up her fork, speared a piece of chicken, then set it back down without eating. "You've been talking to me about marriage for six months. Six months, Cole. But you never actually do anything about it."

The accusation hung between them.

"That's not fair."

"Isn't it?" Her emerald eyes blazed now. "How many times have we had conversations about our future? About building a life together? About kids and a home and everything we want? And yet here you sit in a rental house surrounded by boxes you refuse to unpack, driving a car that seats two people. Not exactly the picture of a man ready to start a family."

Each word landed like a fist in his gut.

"I want those things with you." His voice came out hoarse.

"Do you?" Sydney leaned forward, her hands flat on the table. "Because from where I'm sitting, it looks like you want to keep all your options open. One foot out the door, just in case."

"Just in case what?"

"I don't know, Cole. You tell me." Her voice cracked slightly. "What are you so afraid of?"

Everything. Failing her. Disappointing her. Not being enough. Watching her realize she'd made a mistake choosing him.

The truth clawed at his throat. Audrey. The divorce. The shame. Everything he'd hidden for years from everyone, even Derin.

He could tell her. Right now. Just open his mouth and let it all out. He'd been married. He'd failed. He'd destroyed that marriage with his misplaced priorities and his selfishness. And he was terrified he'd do the same thing to her.

But the words wouldn't come. They stuck in his throat, sealing in the lies.

Sydney's eyes searched his face. Waiting.

The silence stretched.

"Were you going to propose last night?" Her voice dropped to barely above a whisper. "At dinner? On my birthday?"

Cole's heart hammered against his ribs, his eyes darting to the cross hanging around her delicate neck. It taunted him. Accused him of the truth—the same truth Sydney had been saying all evening—that he was lying to himself. That his words and actions did not align.

He had to be honest, at least about this one thing.

"Yes." The word came out rough. "Yes, I planned to propose."

"What happened?" Sydney's hands gripped the edge of the table. "What stopped you? Again?"

Tell her. Tell her about Audrey. Tell her about the failure that defined him. Tell her why he wasn't enough then and might not be enough now.

But what came out instead was worse. So much worse.

"I kept thinking about what you said. About your bio clock. And it freaked me out."

The color drained from Sydney's face. "My bio clock."

Cole kept talking, digging the hole deeper. "You're thirty now, and I know you want kids, and Madison's been talking about it, and there's all this pressure—"

"Stop." She stood abruptly, her chair scraping against the floor. "Just stop."

"Sydney—"

"My bio clock?" Her voice shook. "That's what you're going with? After all this time, that's what you've been afraid of?"

"I didn't say I was afraid—"

"You literally just said it freaked you out." She pressed her palms to her temples. "Do you hear yourself? Do you hear how that sounds?"

Cole stood too, his own chair pushing back. "I'm trying to be honest—"

"Are you?" Sydney's laugh was sharp, bitter. "Because that doesn't sound like honesty. That sounds like an excuse. A really pathetic excuse that reduces me to my ovaries and absolves you of any real responsibility for why you can't commit."

"That's not what I meant."

"Then what did you mean?" She crossed her arms, her whole body rigid. "Because you just told me that the reason you didn't propose on my birthday, the reason you've been stringing me along for six months while talking about marriage, is that you're afraid I want kids. News flash, Cole, we've talked about kids. Multiple times. You knew I wanted them. You said you wanted them too."

He had said that. He *did* want them. With her.

But the fear... The shame…

"I do want kids. With you. I just—"

"You just what?" Sydney's eyes were bright now, whether with tears or anger he couldn't tell. "You just need more time? More time to live in your rental house with your boxes? More time to drive your sports car and pretend you're not building a life here? How much time do you need, Cole?"

"I don't know." The admission came out broken.

Sydney grabbed her purse from the counter, her movements sharp and deliberate. "I know that I'm thirty years old. I know I want to get married and have children. I know that I've been patient and understanding and willing to wait for you to be ready. But I also know that I can't keep doing this."

"Doing what?"

"Waiting for you to decide if I'm worth the risk." Her voice cracked on the last word, and her lip trembled. "Wondering if you're ever going to actually commit or if you're just going to keep me in this holding pattern forever while you figure out if you want to go back to your old life."

"I don't want my old life." That, at least, was honest.

"Then act like it." Sydney's hand was on the doorknob now. "Unpack your boxes. Make this place a home. Trade in the McLaren for something practical. Show me, don't just tell me, that you want this life. That you want me."

"I do want you."

"But you didn't propose." The words fell between them

like stones. "You had the perfect moment. My birthday. Romantic dinner. And you choked. Again. How many times, Cole? How many times have you almost asked me but didn't?"

He couldn't answer that. Couldn't tell her it was five. Five separate occasions over six months where he'd had the ring, had the moment, and let fear win.

Sydney shook her head slowly. "You know what the worst part is? I can see it on your face right now that there's something you're not telling me. Something big. And instead of being honest about whatever it is, you're blaming my bio clock."

His stomach twisted. She could see right through him to the secret he'd buried so deep.

"Sydney, I—"

"Oh, Cole." The way she said his name broke something inside him. Disappointment. Hurt. Resignation. And underneath it all, the dawning realization that he'd just made everything infinitely worse.

"Don't." Her voice was quiet now, deadly calm. "Don't call me. Don't text me. Don't send flowers with some meaningless apology card. I need space to figure out what I'm doing here. What we're doing. If there even is a 'we' anymore."

"Of course there's a—"

"Is there?" She yanked the door open. "Because I thought there was. I thought we were building toward marriage. A lifetime together. But you're not. You're just... waiting. For what? I don't even think you know."

The door closed behind her with a soft click that echoed through the house like a gunshot.

Cole stood frozen in his kitchen, surrounded by unpacked boxes and half-eaten meatloaf, and listened to her car start in the driveway. The engine turned over. Headlights swept across his front window. Then the sound faded into the distance, leaving only silence.

He'd had the chance to tell her the truth.

And he'd chosen a lie instead.

The worst plausible lie. One that made him sound shallow and immature and scared of commitment for all the wrong reasons. One that hurt the woman he loved. The woman who'd waited patiently for him while he worked through fears he refused to unearth.

Cole sank into his chair, his head in his hands. The ring box dug into his hip from his pocket, a constant reminder of every failed proposal. Every missed chance. Every moment he'd let fear win.

Father, what have I done?

But he knew. He knew exactly what he'd done.

He'd lied to the woman he loved rather than tell her the truth about his past.

He'd blamed her age rather than fess up to his own cowardice.

He'd pushed away the best thing in his life because he was too afraid to let her see the worst parts of himself.

The meatloaf sat congealing on his plate. Sydney's Caesar salad, barely touched. Evidence of another ruined evening. Another failure.

Cole looked around the living room. The boxes stacked against the wall, some still taped shut from when he'd moved in last June. The bare walls. The complete lack of anything personal or permanent.

She was right. About all of it.

He was living like a man ready to run. And he didn't even know what he was running from anymore.

No, that was another lie.

He knew exactly what he was running from.

The ghost of a failed marriage. The shame of a divorce he'd told no one about. The fear that if Sydney knew the truth, she'd see him the way he saw himself.

Damaged. Broken. Not worth her love. Or her time.

His phone buzzed in his pocket. For a split second, hope

flared. Maybe it was Sydney. Maybe she'd calmed down enough to—

No. It was Derin.

How'd it go? Did you talk to her?

Cole stared at the message. The woman he loved had just walked out his door and told him not to contact her.

He set the phone face down on the table.

The silence in the house felt different now. Not just empty.

Hollow.

And the boxes lining his walls weren't just unpacked belongings anymore.

They were evidence. Proof that Sydney was right about everything.

He'd been living in fear for so long that he didn't know how to do anything else.

SYDNEY TUGGED THE brush through her hair one more time, staring at her reflection in the bathroom mirror. The silence in her apartment felt heavier than usual this Sunday morning. Three days since she'd walked out of Cole's house. Three days of nothing—no texts, no calls, no accidental run-ins except the careful avoidance dance they'd managed at work on Friday. Saturday had simply been empty. No plans together, no plans to not have plans. Just nothing, stretching from morning to night.

She set down the brush and reached for her earrings, the small silver hoops Cole had given her for her birthday last year. Her fingers hesitated over them before she picked them up anyway. Whatever was broken between them, she still loved him.

That was the problem, wasn't it?

Sydney fastened the earrings and grabbed her purse

from the table by the door. Sunday mornings used to mean Cole picking her up, the two of them driving to church together, sitting side by side during the service. A year of Sundays, of shared routines, of feeling like they were building the foundation for a long, intimate future.

Now she drove herself, and the wrongness of it sat heavy in her heart.

She paused by the door, her hand on the knob, and closed her eyes.

God, I don't understand. I thought Cole was the one. I really believed You were leading me to him. Was I wrong? Did I hear You wrong?

She'd been so sure. A year of dating, of getting to know him, of falling deeper in love with the steady, reliable man who made her laugh and made her feel safe. How could she have been so certain and so wrong at the same time?

She'd taken the job at Vargas Ranch believing God led her here. That this was home. That He was giving her roots, community, and a place to belong. Then Cole had asked her out, and every conversation, every shared moment had felt like confirmation. Like God was writing their love story.

The memory of her thirtieth birthday dinner flashed through her mind. The necklace. Not the ring. Cole's face when she couldn't hide her disappointment.

Had she been wrong about all of it?

Sydney drew a breath and forced herself to keep praying.

I'm thirty years old. I want to be a wife. I want to be a mother. I want babies, Lord. Children to raise in Your ways. A family of my own. But I don't have time to wait forever. I don't have years to spend wondering if Cole is ever going to choose me.

Should she break up with him? Was that what God was asking her to do? She needed wisdom. Desperately. She couldn't keep doing this. Couldn't keep hoping and being disappointed.

The weight of unanswered questions pressed in.

Sydney opened her eyes and reached for the door. Maybe she'd hear something at church.

The drive took fifteen minutes, the same route Cole had driven dozens of times. Every mile felt strange without him next to her, without his quiet presence and the easy conversation they always fell into. Even the sunshine streaming through her windshield felt too bright, too cheerful.

She pulled into the parking lot and found a spot near a row of mesquite trees. Through her windshield, she could see people streaming toward the entrance. Couples walked side by side, families with children.

That was supposed to be her. Supposed to be them.

Sydney grabbed her Bible from the passenger seat and headed inside.

The sanctuary was already half full when she entered. The worship band ran through a sound check on stage, and padded chairs arranged in gentle curves faced the platform. The casual cowboy church vibe always made the space feel welcoming. Boots and jeans mixed with Sunday dresses, the atmosphere relaxed and warm.

Sydney scanned the room and spotted Solana and Renata sitting with their parents about halfway toward the front. Solana caught her eye and waved, patting the empty chair beside her.

No saved seat for Cole.

She started down the aisle. That's when she saw them.

Dalton and River Vargas, three rows from the front. River held one of their twins on her lap. Sloane, maybe, based on the blue outfit. Dalton had the other twin, Elena, perched on his knee. The little girl giggled and reached for her daddy's face, and Dalton smiled down at her with an expression Sydney had no word for except home.

Eighteen months old. Walking, talking, laughing. A family.

That's what I want, Lord. The prayer was barely formed, more ache than words. *A husband at my side and babies in my arms.*

Solana's mother squeezed her hand, and Sydney murmured her hellos and opened her Bible in her lap.

The worship leader stepped up to the microphone, and the band shifted into the opening notes of the first song. Around her, people stood, and Sydney rose with them.

Movement near the back caught her eye.

Cole.

He slipped through the door just as the first verse started, his gaze sweeping the room before he walked quickly down the side aisle. He didn't look in her direction. Instead, he slid into a row across the sanctuary, settling next to Derin and Madison.

Sydney's heart cracked.

Three days of silence, and somewhere in the middle of them she'd started to wonder if she'd ever really known him. The unpacked boxes had rattled something loose in her—not just hurt, but a deeper uncertainty. A year of dating. What else hadn't she known? What else was he hiding, waiting for the right moment that never seemed to come?

But then she actually looked at him.

The rumpled shirt. The way his shoulders sat forward, like something heavy had settled across them and he'd stopped trying to shake it off. Cole kept his beard neat with clean edges, never careless. This morning the lines had gone soft, the edges untended. She'd noticed early on the way he carried himself, the quiet effort he put into his appearance. Small things, but they added up to a man who was always present, always polished.

This was not that man.

She knew him well enough to understand what she was seeing. Cole didn't wear his feelings. Never had. So when they showed up on the outside like this, it meant whatever he was carrying had gotten too heavy to hide.

The impulse to cross the sanctuary hit her before she could stop it. Just go to him. Sit down next to him. Let him know she was still there.

But she caught herself. She didn't know what she'd be walking toward. That was the entire problem—she still didn't know. And she couldn't keep reaching for someone who hadn't yet chosen to let her in.

She couldn't fix this. She didn't even fully understand it.

Please help him, Lord. Whatever he's carrying – whatever he's been carrying all this time – please help him.

She dragged her gaze back to the screen and forced herself to focus on the words of the song. But the lyrics blurred, and all she could see was Cole sitting across the sanctuary, so close and yet impossibly far away.

This wasn't how it was supposed to be.

The service continued. Sydney heard pieces of it, caught fragments. But mostly she was aware of the space between her and Cole, the physical distance that mirrored everything broken between them.

When the pastor stepped up to the platform, she tried to focus. She was so tired of the questions churning in her own mind. Maybe someone else's words would quiet them.

He opened his Bible to 1 Kings 17. The widow of Zarephath, he said. A woman who had lost everything—her husband gone, her resources nearly spent, and the famine grinding on with no end in sight. She'd gone out to gather a few sticks to make a fire. One last meal for herself and her son before they starved. No prayer for rescue. No expectation of anything changing. Just a woman doing the last thing she had left to do, because that was all there was.

And God had sent Elijah to her door.

Not until the flour almost ran out. Not before she'd already gathered the sticks and resigned herself to the end. In the very moment of it, when hope had already folded.

Sydney stilled.

"Sometimes," Pastor Jared said, "we can't see what is on the other side of waiting. We don't know if a miracle is coming or not. But He still asks us to wait. To trust. And sometimes the miracle is the waiting."

The words landed somewhere beneath her breastbone and stayed there, quiet and immovable.

She wasn't the widow. She knew that. But the shape of it was the same—the feeling that time was running out, that she had nothing left to give the waiting, that if something didn't change soon, there would be nothing left of her hope to spend.

And still He asked.

She bowed her head. Not with answers. Just with the weight of it.

The worship band started the final song, a slower melody that invited reflection. Sydney stood with everyone else, her hands loose at her sides, and let the music wash over her. Around her, voices lifted in quiet harmony, and for a moment the exhaustion in her shoulders loosened its grip.

She closed her eyes, shutting out the sanctuary, the people, the pull toward Cole across the room.

She was so tired of not knowing. Tired of holding the uncertainty at arm's length, examining it from every angle, trying to force it into something she could act on. She didn't have the strength for another round of the same questions.

And in the middle of that exhaustion, in the space between one breath and the next, something settled.

Not an audible voice. Not a verse flashing through her mind. Just a single word, gentle and unmistakable.

Wait.

How long, Lord? What am I waiting for?

Just wait.

Not a command that felt harsh or dismissive. Just—wait. Be still. Trust Him. The widow hadn't known what was on the other side of the waiting either.

Sydney opened her eyes, blinking back tears. The song ended, and the pastor offered a closing prayer. She bowed her head, her heart still turning over that single word.

Even as the confusion swirled, something eased. No

clarity about Cole or her future or what came next. Just enough peace to trust and obey, even when she didn't understand.

She wasn't supposed to decide anything right now. She was supposed to wait.

And pray.

The service dismissed, and people began to gather their things. Solana touched her arm, asking if she wanted to grab lunch, but Sydney shook her head.

"I think I need some time alone," she said.

Solana squeezed her hand and let her go.

Sydney gathered her Bible and purse and stood. Across the sanctuary, Cole stood too, moving toward the side exit with his head down, his steps quick.

He didn't look back.

She watched him go, the ache in her chest sharpening. Then she walked toward the exit, her steps slow, letting the crowd carry her forward.

She reached the parking lot and paused, blinking in the bright Arizona sunshine. Her car sat in the back row of the parking lot, alone. No Cole waiting to drive her home. No shared lunch plans. No casual conversation about the sermon or what they'd do with the rest of their Sunday.

Just her.

And God's quiet instruction to wait.

Sydney unlocked her car and slid into the driver's seat. She gripped the steering wheel and stared through the windshield at nothing.

I will wait, Lord. But please – show me what I'm waiting for.

She started the engine and pulled out of the parking lot, heading back toward the ranch.

The drive back to the ranch took her along the familiar stretch of road where the desert opened up on both sides, saguaros standing quiet in the midmorning light. In the distance, Dalton Peak rose against the pale sky, the same as always. The same as it had been every Sunday morning she'd driven this road. Solid. Unchanged. Indifferent to the particular troubles of one woman in a compact car with a Bible on the passenger seat.

It had been waiting there long before she arrived. It would be waiting long after.

She exhaled slowly.

She would wait. And she would pray.

5

COLE ARRIVED AT the office Monday morning to find Derin waiting outside, two steaming mugs in hand.

Just what he needed. An audience.

He'd come in early hoping to bury himself in work before anyone else showed up. Before he had to face questions he couldn't answer. Four days since Thursday night, and the weight of Sydney's absence pressed heavier with each passing hour.

"Thought you could use this." Derin extended one mug, his tone casual. Too casual.

Cole accepted it, the warmth seeping into his palms doing nothing to thaw the cold knot in his chest. "Thanks."

They stood in silence. Derin's gaze drifted to the distant mountains, but Cole felt the weight of his friend's attention. Studying. Assessing. Derin had always been perceptive—too perceptive sometimes—and Cole had no doubt his current state registered loud and clear.

He took a sip. Black, the way he liked it. Derin knew that. After six years of friendship, Derin knew a lot of things. Maybe too many things.

But not everything. Not the one thing that mattered most.

"Remember that camping trip?" Derin said, still watching the sunrise paint the sky in shades of orange and pink.

"Six years ago?"

The question came out casual, but Cole's gut clenched. Yeah, he remembered the camping trip that had saved his life—or at least kept him from completely falling apart after the divorce papers were finalized.

"Hard to forget," Cole managed. "Your brothers rigged that straw draw."

"Stuck me with some corporate type." Derin's chuckle held a trace of nostalgia. "You were a mess, but you gave everything two hundred percent. Never shied away from the hard stuff."

The hard stuff. Like sleeping on the ground when his back was killing him. Like chopping wood when his hands were already blistered. Like talking about faith when his world had just crumbled.

Cole stared into his mug, watching steam curl upward and disappear. That camping trip had been a turning point. Three days away from everything, two nights under stars so bright. Never seen anything like it. Derin had been younger, cocky in that way twenty-somethings could be when they thought they had life figured out. Cole had been older but no wiser, running from failure and shame.

Somehow they'd found common ground.

"Best thing that could've happened," Derin said.

Cole's jaw clenched. He knew where this was going. Derin didn't reminisce without reason.

"Time in nature clears your head." Derin finally turned to face him.

There it was. Derin had seen something. Probably seen everything, knowing him. The failed proposal. Sydney's absence. Cole's carefully constructed life as it unraveled at the seams.

Cole forced himself to meet Derin's gaze. "You planning another camping trip?"

"Yeah. Couple of weeks. For our guys rehabbing here. The athletes who are so focused on their bodies that they forget about the rest." Derin paused. "Want you to plan it. I was thinking we'll bring Adan and Ross."

Cole's stomach tightened. Adan, who'd found redemption after his injury ended his PBR career. Ross, one of the newer cowboys who'd been quietly proving himself around the ranch. Both of them solid men who didn't hide who they were.

And Cole, who'd built his entire life around a lie.

Cold dread pooled in Cole's stomach. A camping trip. The truth had a way of popping up in that kind of environment, whether or not you were ready for it.

That's what had happened six years ago, hadn't it? He'd told Derin everything about the career that was killing him, about needing to change his life. Everything except the one truth that mattered most.

And now Derin was inviting him into that space again. With other broken men. Men who'd probably share their wounds openly while Cole sat there choking on his secret.

He could go. Keep his mouth shut. Preserve the lie he'd built so carefully. No reason the truth had to come out. They'd talk about injuries and rehab and getting back in the game. Physical stuff. Safe stuff.

Except it wouldn't be safe. Not with Derin steering the conversation toward things Cole had been avoiding for years.

His hand tightened around the coffee mug. Part of him wanted to say no. Make an excuse. Protect himself the way he always did.

But another part—the part that had been suffocating under the weight of lies—whispered that maybe this was exactly what he needed. Space away from Sydney's wounded eyes and his own cowardice. A chance to breathe without the constant pressure of maintaining his facade.

Maybe he could finally stop thinking about her all day, every day. Stop replaying Thursday night on an endless loop. Stop feeling the phantom weight of the ring box in his pocket.

Or maybe he'd crack wide open and lose the last shred of control he had left.

"Two weeks out?" he mumbled as tension bunched his shoulders.

"That's what I was thinking. You, Adan, Ross—meet this afternoon at two to plan. Nothing strenuous. Adapted for guys still recovering."

Planning. Logistics. Coordinating schedules and supplies. Concrete tasks with measurable outcomes.

Things he excelled at.

Not like emotions. Not like relationships. Not like watching Sydney's face crumble when she had looked at those unpacked boxes Thursday night.

You say you want to put down roots, embrace this slower life, but you haven't even moved into it yet.

Her words had carved themselves into his brain. She'd quoted Jeremiah at him. *The heart is deceitful above all else.* Like she could see straight through him to the lies he'd been telling himself.

Maybe she could. Maybe that's what scared him most.

"I'll do it," he said.

Derin's expression softened, just a fraction. Relief, maybe. Or understanding. "Good. I'll let the others know."

They stood there in the growing light, the morning air still cool despite the climbing sun. Somewhere in the distance, horses whinnied. The ranch was waking up, starting another day as if nothing had changed.

But everything had changed. Sydney had called him out, and he had let her walk away rather than tell her the truth.

Cole knew he should say something. Acknowledge what Derin was really offering—not just a camping trip but a lifeline. A chance to step away from the wreckage and figure out what came next.

But the words tangled in his throat the way they always did when the personal stakes were so high. When Audrey had asked him what was wrong in their marriage, he'd deflected. When his parents had questioned his career change, he smiled and changed the subject. When Sydney had asked why he hadn't unpacked, he'd given her excuses.

He was a master at avoiding the conversations that counted.

"Thanks for the coffee," he finally managed.

Derin studied him for another long moment, and Cole had the uncomfortable feeling his friend could read every thought racing through his head. But Derin just nodded and clapped him on the shoulder.

"Anytime, bro."

As Derin walked away, Cole remained where he was, staring into the dregs of his coffee. Time in nature. Clearing his head. Putting things into perspective.

It had worked before. That camping trip six years ago, when he felt like his entire life was imploding. Three days away from everything had given him space to breathe. To pray. To remember that God's plans weren't always the same as his own plans, and that sometimes failure wasn't the end of the story.

Maybe that's what he needed now. Space to figure out why he could face down difficult negotiations with million-dollar clients but couldn't unpack boxes in his own home. Why he could help athletes navigate career-ending injuries but couldn't navigate his own heart.

The office was quiet, just the hum of the computer and the ticking of the clock on the wall. Cole set his mug down and pulled out his phone to text Adan and Ross about the planning meeting.

His thumb hovered over Sydney's name in his contacts.

Four days. They'd gone four days without talking, the longest silence since they'd started dating over a year ago. He'd seen her at church Sunday morning, sitting three rows ahead with her roommates. She hadn't turned around. Hadn't acknowledged him.

And he'd been too cowardly to approach her.

The heart is deceitful above all else.

Cole grabbed his phone and shoved it in his pocket. He had a camping trip to plan. Work to do. Athletes who needed his expertise and attention.

And the thought of spending two nights under the stars with men who wouldn't let him hide terrified him more than he wanted to admit.

SYDNEY'S MONDAY STARTED with paperwork that refused to make sense no matter how many times she read the same paragraph.

She gave up and shoved the intake forms aside, rubbing her temples. Four days since she'd walked out of Cole's house, and her brain still couldn't focus on anything beyond the image of those boxes. Packed. Ready to leave. After months of claiming he wanted to put down roots.

The heart is deceitful above all else.

She'd thrown Jeremiah at him like a weapon, but the verse had lodged in her mind too. Was her heart deceiving her? Had she been wrong about Cole, about them, about what God wanted for her life?

The questions circled endlessly, wearing grooves in her mind.

A knock on her office door pulled her from the spiral.

"Come in."

Madison poked her head inside, her smile cautious. "You okay?"

"Fine." She sighed.

"You've been staring at that same page for twenty minutes." Madison stepped fully into the office, closing the door behind her. "I could see you from the hallway."

Sydney managed a weak smile. "Guess I'm a little distracted."

"A little." Madison settled into the chair across from her desk. "Derin told me about the camping idea. Said Cole's coordinating it."

Of course he was. Cole always threw himself into work when things got difficult. It was easier than dealing with emotions, than having hard conversations, than unpacking boxes that might force him to admit he lived here.

"Good for him," Sydney said.

Madison's expression softened. "Syd—"

"I'm fine. Really." She straightened in her chair, reaching for her professional mask. "What can I help you with?"

For a moment, Madison looked like she might push. Then she sighed and shifted gears. "We have a new guest arriving this morning. Luca Marchetti."

The name sparked recognition. "Luca? From the tour?"

"You remember him?"

"Of course I do." Sydney felt the first genuine interest she'd experienced in days. "Italian player, incredible serve. He was at the US Open when—" She stopped, the memory of Madison's injury still tender even two years later.

"When my shoulder ligament tore." Madison's voice was matter-of-fact. "Yeah. He was there. Came to visit me in Colorado afterward, actually. Brought flowers."

Sydney remembered that day with painful clarity. September heat and the sound of Madison's scream echoing across the court. The ambulance. The chaos. And later, after Madison had surgery back home in Colorado, a steady stream of players and coaches offering support.

Luca had been one of them.

"What's he coming in for?" Sydney asked.

"Shoulder injury. Not as severe as mine was, but he wants to finish his rehab somewhere quiet. Away from the press and the tour atmosphere." Madison glanced at her watch. "He should arrive any minute, actually. I thought you might want to be there when he checks in. You knew his old PA, didn't you?"

"Giuliana?" Sydney's mind flashed to the efficient Italian woman who'd kept Luca's schedule running like clockwork. "She got married last year. Moved to Milan, I think."

"That's what Luca said in his intake forms. He's been managing without an assistant since then." Madison stood. "Come on. Let's go meet him."

Sydney followed her friend through the corridors of the guest ranch, past the main dining hall and out toward the arrival courtyard. The morning sun had burned off the early coolness, and heat was already building.

A black SUV pulled up as they approached, the driver emerging to open the back passenger door.

And there was Luca Marchetti, just as she remembered him. Tall and lean, dark hair styled with casual European flair, designer sunglasses perched on his nose. He wore linen pants and a crisp white shirt with the sleeves rolled up, looking more like he was arriving at a Mediterranean resort than an Arizona guest ranch.

He saw Madison first and broke into a wide smile.

"Madison!" He strode forward, and Sydney watched Madison brace for impact as Luca pulled her into an enthusiastic hug, kissing both her cheeks. "You look wonderful. Marriage agrees with you, yes?"

"It does." Madison laughed, gently extricating herself. "Luca, it's good to see you."

"I was so sad when you retired." His expression turned somber for a moment. "You had so much more to give to the game. But I understand. The injury, it was bad."

"It was time," Madison said. "And I found something better here."

"Better than tennis?" Luca's eyebrow arched, but his smile returned. "You must show me this better thing."

"I will." Madison stepped back, gesturing to Sydney. "You remember—"

"Sydney!" Luca's face lit up with genuine delight. "Of

course I remember. How could I forget Madison's right hand? The woman who kept everything running smoothly even when you were being, how do you say, the diva?"

"I was not a diva," Madison protested, but she was grinning.

"You were a little bit diva." Luca turned his full attention to Sydney, pulling her into the same enthusiastic embrace, complete with kisses on both cheeks. "Ciao, bella. It has been too long."

The familiar greeting, the warmth of his manner, the faint scent of expensive cologne—it all transported Sydney back to a different life. Airport lounges and five-star hotels. Press conferences and championship matches. The constant movement, the adrenaline, the electricity of being part of something bigger.

She'd given it all up for this quiet ranch in Arizona. For sports rehabilitation and intake forms and a man who couldn't even unpack his boxes.

"It's good to see you, Luca." She stepped back, reclaiming her professional space. "Welcome to Vargas Ranch."

"This place." He turned in a slow circle, taking in the desert landscape, the mountains in the distance, the rustic-meets-luxury aesthetic of the ranch buildings. "It is not what I expected. When Madison told me about this, I thought, what? She is hiding in the desert? But now I see. It has a certain... charm."

"Wait until you see the sports rehabilitation facility," Sydney said. "That's really the heart of what we do here at Vargas Sports."

"Ah, this is why Madison speaks so highly of this place." Luca's expression turned thoughtful. "Working with athletes who understand what it is like. The fear. The uncertainty."

"Exactly," Madison said. "The program is designed to support your physical therapy while addressing the mental and emotional aspects of recovery."

"Ah yes. The mental aspects." Luca's smile turned rueful. "That is why I am here, if I am honest. The shoulder, it will heal. But the mind? The mind keeps asking, what if this is the end? What if I cannot come back?"

Sydney knew those questions. She'd heard them from dozens of athletes over the years. The fear that lived underneath every injury, every setback. The terror of losing the identity you'd built your entire life around.

She'd watched Madison wrestle with those same fears two years ago.

"You're in the right place," she said quietly. "I promise."

Luca met her eyes, and something shifted in his expression. Recognition, maybe. Or understanding. "You left the tour. Madison told me. I wondered why. You were so good at your job."

The words surprised her. She had been good at her job. Excellent, even. She loved the travel, the challenge, the constant motion. Until she realized the motion was all she had. Until she'd come to Vargas Ranch and discovered something different.

Until she'd met Cole and thought maybe, finally, she'd found where she belonged.

"I found something better," she said, willing herself to believe it.

"Better than the tour?" Luca's eyebrow arched. "What could be better than seeing the world, working with the best athletes?"

"Peace," Madison interjected. "Right, Syd?"

"Right." But the word came out less certain than she intended.

Luca studied her for a long moment, his expression thoughtful. Then he smiled, bright and easy. "Well, I am glad to have you here. Makes me feel less, how do you say, like a fish out of water?"

"You'll settle in quickly," Sydney assured him. "Let's get you checked in and I'll show you to your casita."

The driver had already unloaded Luca's luggage—designer bags that looked ridiculously out of place against the rustic ranch backdrop. Sydney grabbed the lightest one before Luca could protest.

"I can carry that," he said.

"Ranch hospitality," she countered. "Besides, you're supposed to be taking it easy on that shoulder."

"So bossy. I remember this about you." But he was grinning as he fell into step beside her, Madison trailing behind.

As they walked toward the guest casitas, Luca kept up a steady stream of conversation. Updates from the tour. Who was playing well, and who was struggling. Gossip about coaches and sponsors and the eternal drama of professional tennis.

Sydney relaxed into the familiar rhythm. This was a world she understood. A world where the rules were clear and success was measurable. Win or lose. Rank up or rank down. Simple.

Not like relationships. Not like love. Not like trying to build a life with someone who kept one foot out the door.

"Giuliana, she sends her regards," Luca said as they reached his casita. "She is very happy in Milan with her husband. Three months pregnant now."

"That's wonderful." Sydney unlocked the door and gestured him inside. "I'm happy for her."

"She was a good assistant. The best I ever had." Luca set his bags down in the spacious living area, turning to survey the casita. "But she wanted different things. Marriage. Babies. The quiet life."

Something in his tone made Sydney glance up. "Do you miss her? As your assistant, I mean."

"Every day." He moved to the windows overlooking the desert landscape. "I have tried three replacements. None of them understand how I work. None of them anticipate what I need before I need it. It is exhausting."

Sydney understood. The relationship between an athlete and their personal assistant was unique. Part employee, part confidant, part mind reader. When it worked, it was seamless. When it didn't...

"You'll find someone," she said.

Luca turned from the window, his expression casual but his words weighted. "If you ever want to leave this place..."

The suggestion hung in the air, vague enough to be dismissed but specific enough to be understood.

"The ranch has a full schedule of activities," Madison cut in, her voice professionally bright. "We'll set up your initial assessment this afternoon, and then Sydney can show you the sports facility."

"Perfect." Luca's smile returned, easy and charming. "But first, I think I will rest. The travel, it was long."

They left him to settle in, walking back toward the main buildings in silence. Sydney could feel Madison watching her, but she kept her eyes forward.

"He seems good," Sydney finally said.

"He's always been good at putting on a show." Madison's voice held a note of caution. "But Syd, that thing he said about leaving this place—"

"Was just conversation."

"Was it?"

Sydney stopped walking, turning to face her friend. "What are you asking me?"

Madison's expression softened. "I'm asking if you're okay. Because bringing Luca here, having him remind you of everything you left behind... I don't want to make things harder for you."

"Things are already hard." The admission escaped before Sydney could stop it. "Cole and I, we're... I don't even know what we are anymore."

"I know." Madison reached out, squeezing her hand. "Derin told me Cole's been a mess. Whatever happened Thursday night—"

"I saw his house." Sydney's throat tightened. "He hasn't unpacked, Madison. Months after your wedding, and he's still in boxes. Like he's ready to leave any second."

"Maybe he just needs a push to fully commit."

"Or maybe he's been telling me what I wanted to hear while planning his exit strategy." Sydney straightened her back, crossing her arms. "The heart is deceitful, right? Maybe I've been deceiving myself about all of it."

Madison was quiet for a moment. "Or maybe you're both scared and neither of you knows how to say it."

Before Sydney could respond, movement caught her eye. Cole, emerging from the Vargas Sports building, his shoulders tense and his expression dark.

He saw them. Saw her. His stride faltered for just a second before he continued walking, his path carrying him past them toward the parking area.

Sydney's heart lurched. She wanted to call out to him. Wanted to run after him and demand answers. Wanted to shake him until he finally, finally told her the truth about whatever he was hiding.

But she stayed rooted in place, watching him walk away.

Just like she had on Thursday night.

Just like he'd let her.

"Syd—" Madison started.

"I should get back to work." Sydney turned toward her office, needing distance. Needing space to breathe. "Luca's assessment won't schedule itself."

She had made it three steps before she heard it. A cheerful voice calling out in accented English.

"Sydney! Wait!"

She turned to see Luca jogging toward them, his earlier exhaustion apparently forgotten. He reached them slightly breathless, his smile bright.

"I forgot to ask," he said. "Do you have dinner plans tonight? I would love to catch up. Talk about the old days, yes?"

Out of the corner of her eye, Sydney saw Cole. He'd

stopped walking and turned back, watching them. Even from this distance, she could see the tension in his shoulders, the set of his jaw.

"I don't think—" she started.

"Come now. For old times' sake. There is a restaurant in town. Derin mentioned it. I will make reservations." Luca's expression turned playful. "Unless you are too busy with your cowboy life to have dinner with an old friend?"

The challenge was gentle but unmistakable. And something in Sydney—some part of her that was tired of being patient, tired of waiting, tired of watching Cole run away—responded.

"Dinner sounds nice," she said.

Luca's smile widened. "Perfecto. I will text you the details, yes?"

"Sure."

He leaned in, kissing both her cheeks again. "Ciao, Bella. Until tonight."

As he walked back toward his casita, Sydney turned to find Cole still standing there. Still watching. Scowling and pained.

Their eyes met across the distance.

She waited for him to come over. To say something. To finally break the silence that had stretched between them for four endless days.

But Cole just stood there, his hands clenched at his sides, his face a mask of barely controlled emotion.

And then he turned and walked away.

Again.

Sydney watched him go, her heart sinking. Four days of silence. Ten months of unpacked boxes. And now, when faced with the sight of another man paying attention to her, all Cole could do was frown and storm off.

Would he finally break the silence now? Or would this just be more of the same—Cole retreating, avoiding, keeping her at arm's length while claiming he wanted a future together?

"Syd?" Madison's voice was gentle. "You okay?"

"I don't know." The honest answer felt like defeat. "I really don't know."

A traitorous thought whispered through her mind. If things stayed this way—this awkward, painful stalemate—she might have to leave Vargas Ranch. Find a job somewhere else. Maybe in Wickenburg. Something local, where she could still put down roots, still build the settled life she'd dreamed of when she left the tour behind.

But even as the thought formed, that familiar inner voice spoke. The one that had guided her to Arizona in the first place. The one that had confirmed Cole was meant to be her husband.

Wait.

She'd heard it before, when she'd wanted to push for answers Cole wasn't ready to give. When she'd wanted to force the relationship forward faster than it was moving.

And now, watching Cole's retreating back, feeling the ache of his continued silence, she heard it again.

Wait.

Sydney closed her eyes, breathing deeply. She didn't want to wait. She wanted resolution. Wanted answers. Wanted Cole to finally be honest with her about whatever he was hiding.

But God had never steered her wrong before.

Even when He asked her to do the hardest thing of all.

"Come on," Madison said softly, linking her arm through Sydney's. "Let's get back inside. You have work to do, and I have a husband who's probably already texted me three times wondering where I am."

Sydney walked back toward the offices, but she couldn't resist one last glance over her shoulder.

Cole had disappeared around the corner of the building.

Still running. Still hiding.

Still breaking her heart one silent day at a time.

But she was certain God was asking her to wait.

So she would.

Even though she still did not know what she was waiting for.

6

HE STILL WASN'T enough. Not for Sydney. Not if the little scene he'd just witnessed was true.

Cole stuffed his hands deep into his pockets, veering away from the dining hall toward the quiet path along the edge of the resort. The one that skirted the property boundary where guests rarely wandered. He wasn't hungry anymore. His stomach had twisted into a knot the moment he'd seen that tennis player lean close to Sydney, all easy confidence and European charm.

Dalton Peak stood proud against the midday sun, stretching high toward the breathtaking blue sky. The kind of Arizona day that made tourists reach for their cameras. Cole barely registered it. Heat radiated off the gravel path. Sweat gathered at his collar despite the dry air. He couldn't get a full breath.

No. He had to be mistaken. Sydney would never cheat on him. She wasn't like that. Maybe it was an innocent dinner between old friends. Professional. The tennis world was small. They'd worked together before.

He shook his head, boots scuffing against the gravel. Or maybe, if he'd read Luca's interest correctly, it was more.

The man's easy confidence had said everything. The way he'd touched Sydney's arm. Held her gaze a beat too long. Gravitas Cole recognized immediately, having negotiated contracts with men like that for years.

Cole's jaw tightened. Not because Luca was dangerous. He probably wasn't. But because Sydney had smiled back.

Not the polite, professional smile she gave difficult athletes. A genuine smile. Warm. Like she used to give Cole before he'd spent months letting her down with five failed proposals.

That was the problem. Not Luca.

Him.

He stopped walking and turned back toward the main buildings. He should go back there. Ask her directly what that was about. Confront Luca if he had to.

Cole's hands curled into fists at his side.

And say what? He had no right to be possessive when he couldn't even commit.

He forced himself to turn around. Keep walking. The path stretched ahead, empty and quiet. Cooler in the shade of well-manicured palo verde trees.

Why wouldn't she be interested in Luca? The man was everything Cole wasn't. Younger, probably by five years. Successful in a way that made headlines. Not dragging around the baggage of a failed marriage like an anchor tied to his ankles. A man who committed without choking on his own fear.

A man who deserved someone like Sydney.

Cole stopped again, this time bracing one hand against the smooth bark of a palo verde. The desert landscape blurred in front of him. Saguaros dotted the hillside like sentries. Ocotillo branches reached toward the cloudless sky, their tips crowned with scarlet blooms. Beautiful. Peaceful. Everything he'd moved here to find.

And he was losing it all because he couldn't get out of his own way.

A gecko skittered across the path, stopping for a few push-ups, which normally would have made him laugh. Then it disappeared into a crack between rocks. Cole watched it go, envying its ability to vanish.

His phone buzzed in his pocket. He ignored it. Probably work. The sports complex didn't stop operating just because his life imploded around him. Again.

The familiar spiral started. The one that had kept him awake every night since Sydney's birthday. He'd broken something that night. Something that might not be fixable. She'd seen the coward who couldn't commit. More than a year of her life wasted on a man who would never be what she expected.

His stomach churned. The image of her smile flashed through his mind. The way she'd leaned in when Luca spoke. She'd pulled back from Cole. Stopped texting him good morning. Stopped suggesting they grab coffee between meetings. Stopped looking at him the way she used to.

Cole pushed off the tree, forcing his feet to move. The path curved toward the employee parking area. His McLaren gleamed in the sun, lime green and completely impractical. Two seats. No room for car seats or groceries, or anything permanent. Just like the rest of his life.

He should have traded it in months ago. Should have proposed at Christmas. Should have been honest with Sydney from the beginning.

Should have told her about his first wife.

The thought hit like a fist to his gut. There it was. The truth he couldn't outrun no matter how far he ran or how hard he worked. He'd failed before. Spectacularly. And now he failed again, right on schedule. Different woman. Same pattern. Same coward hiding behind the same excuses.

His ex-wife had found someone better. A youth pastor who prioritized her. Who showed up. Who didn't hide behind work and fear and a secret he was too ashamed to share. She had three kids now. The family life Cole had never given her. The future he'd promised and then destroyed.

And Sydney? She deserved better too. Maybe Luca Marchetti could be that.

Two weeks after their first double dinner date at Derin's place—the one where Derin's mom had brought over those amazing churros—Cole had finally worked up the courage to ask Sydney to dinner. Just the two of them. Right before Madison retired from tennis and Sydney joined Vargas Sports.

She'd looked perfect that night. Navy dress that brought out something warm in her eyes. Hair down instead of pulled back like she wore it for work. The hostess had seated them by the window, and the sunset had painted everything gold.

The conversation flowed easily between them, the way it always did. Career dreams. Favorite books. Childhood stories that made them both laugh. She told him about growing up in Iowa and how she'd always wanted to see the desert. He told her about his college days, carefully editing out the parts about his marriage.

When dessert arrived, he knew he could fall for Sydney in a way that terrified him.

The drive back to the ranch had been quieter. Not awkward. Just weighted with possibility. He'd walked her to the door of the six-room casita where she had been staying, his pulse hammering like it had as teenager.

In the dim light of the porch, her eyes had beckoned him forward. No games. No pretense. Just Sydney looking at him like she wanted exactly what he wanted.

He'd kissed her. Finally. Softly at first, then deeper when she leaned into him. Her hand had come up to rest against his chest, right over his racing heart. She had tasted like the chocolate mousse they had shared. Sweet. Perfect.

When they'd pulled apart, she'd smiled. That genuine smile of hers that stirred dreams he'd left behind long ago.

"Took you long enough," she'd whispered.

He'd laughed, full of relief and joy and something that felt dangerously close to hope. "Worth the wait?"

"Absolutely."

A car door slammed in the parking lot, jerking Cole back to the present. He blinked, the memory dissolving like smoke. His throat tightened. *Absolutely.* She'd said absolutely then. Said yes to him without hesitation. Without fear. Without expecting him to be anyone other than who he was.

Or who she thought he was.

What would she say now, more than a year later? No ring. Just a necklace and empty words. And Luca right there, ready to become everything Cole couldn't.

His phone buzzed again. This time he pulled it out. Text from Adan: *Meeting in 30. Your office?*

Right. The camping trip planning meeting. The one Derin had asked him to coordinate. Real life continued even as Cole's world shattered around him.

He typed back: *See you then.*

Professional. Competent. The persona he could still maintain even when everything inside him was dying. He'd perfected this skill over years of hiding. Smile. Perform. Keep the secret buried. Let no one see the failure underneath.

Cole pocketed his phone and headed back toward his office at the sports complex. The walk took him through the main training room. Athletes worked through their rehabilitation routines under Ryan's watchful eye. The weight room he'd designed. The recovery center that had helped dozens of injured athletes return to their sport. The counseling that helped others prepare for a new career.

Everything he'd accomplished here. Everything he was good at.

None of it mattered if he lost Sydney.

Back in his office, Cole pulled up the document he'd started for the camping trip. Notes from his conversation with Derin. Ideas about giving the athletes an authentic cowboy roundup experience while accommodating their injuries. Maps of potential campsites on ranch land.

Problems he could actually solve.

A knock on his doorframe interrupted his thoughts. Adan Franco stood there, cowboy hat in hand, the easy confidence of a former PBR world champion mixed with the humility of a man who'd found redemption. Behind him, Ross Braxton—one of the newer cowboys at the ranch, still proving himself but already earning respect through hard work.

"Come in." Cole gestured to the chairs across from his desk. "Thanks for making time."

"No problem." Adan settled into a seat, Ross taking the other. "Derin said you wanted to plan something special for the athletes."

Cole pulled up his notes on the computer screen, then rotated the monitor so they could all see. "He wants to give them an authentic cowboy experience. Something that captures what a real roundup would be like, but adapted for people dealing with injuries."

Ross leaned forward, studying the screen. "That's a tall order. Real roundup work tears you up physically."

"Which is why I need your input." Cole clicked through to his activity list. "I'm thinking less about the actual cattle work and more about the authentic cowboy experience. Camp life. Skills. Something that shows them a lifestyle they've never known."

Adan nodded. "Teach them what cowboys actually do beyond just herding cattle."

"Exactly." Cole switched into operations mode. "What would you include if you wanted to give someone a real taste of the cowboy life?"

"Roping." Adan leaned back in his chair. "Set up stationary targets. They get the feel of the rope, the technique, without having to chase anything down."

Ross nodded. "Camp cooking. Dutch oven meals, coffee over an open fire. Food tastes different outdoors."

Cole made notes, his hands moving automatically. This he could do. Plan. Coordinate. Solve problems. "What about skill demonstrations? Things they can try even with limited mobility?"

"Horse care," Adan said. "Grooming, tack work. Gives them hands-on time with the animals without the physical demands of riding."

"Knot work," Ross added. "Basic equipment care. Fire building without matches—that one always gets them."

They spent the next twenty minutes brainstorming. Cole contributed ideas about adapting activities for different injury levels. Adan proposed working with the horses. Ross offered practical ideas about what they could safely do.

He could still do this. Still function. Still be the guy everyone depended on.

"What about the route?" Cole pulled up the topographical map. "I'm thinking three days, two nights. Needs to be challenging enough to feel authentic but manageable."

Ross leaned closer, studying the terrain. "Here to here." He traced a path with his finger. "Natural water sources, good camping spots. Terrain'll make them work without breaking them."

Cole marked the route. His mind operated on autopilot, professional habits taking over. Schedule planning. Equipment lists. Staff coordination.

All the things he was good at.

Not emotions. Not relationships. Not watching Sydney's face crumble when she looked at those unpacked boxes Thursday night.

She was right. He had said he wanted to put down roots and embrace the western lifestyle, but he hadn't even moved into it yet.

"Cole?" Ross's voice cut through his thoughts. "You still with us?"

"Yeah." Cole looked up. Both men watched him cautiously. They'd noticed he was off. "Just thinking through the plan."

Adan's eyes narrowed slightly, that same perceptive

look Derin got sometimes. Like he could sense something was wrong even if he couldn't pinpoint what.

"You okay, man?" Ross asked quietly. "You seem distracted."

Cole forced confidence into his posture, straightening in his chair. "Just a lot on my plate. You know how it is."

Neither man looked convinced, but they didn't push. Adan glanced at Ross, some silent communication passing between them, then back to Cole.

"Well, if you need anything," Adan said carefully, "we're around."

"Thanks. I appreciate it." Cole pulled the conversation back to safer ground. "So for the campfire, I was thinking Derin could share real roundup stories. Give the athletes that connection to ranch history."

They discussed a few more details. Cole contributed where needed.

Finally, they stood to leave.

"This is going to be good," Ross said, settling his hat back on his head. "These guys need this. Time away from everything, clear their heads."

That's what Derin had said. Like he knew exactly what Cole needed.

"Yeah," Cole managed. "Should be good."

After they left, he stayed at his desk, staring at his screen. Three days, two nights. Men being vulnerable under the stars. Sharing their stories. Their failures. Their fears.

And Cole, sitting there with his secret locked tight. Keeping the lie going. Preserving the facade.

His throat tightened with something that felt like both terror and relief.

He closed the document and stood, grabbing his keys from the desk. The afternoon stretched ahead of him, hollow. Work he should do. Calls he should make. A house he should go home to. Boxes he ought to unpack.

Instead, all he could see was Sydney's smile. The way

Luca had leaned in. The future slipping away because Cole couldn't get unstuck from his past. Now it threatened his dreams.

He still wasn't enough.

And now Sydney might finally realize it too.

The knot in his stomach tightened. He couldn't catch his breath.

He'd lost her before he'd ever really had her.

Because he was too much of a coward to fight for what he wanted.

SYDNEY STARED AT the spreadsheet on her computer screen, the numbers blurring together until they meant nothing. She blinked, trying to refocus on the quarterly budget analysis she was supposed to be reviewing, but her mind refused to cooperate.

Outside her office window, clouds gathered over the mountains. White and puffy, innocent-looking to anyone who hadn't lived through an Arizona summer. But Sydney knew better now. Those clouds meant rain was coming, probably within the hour.

She sighed.

It had been two weeks since she and Cole had last talked. Two weeks of careful avoidance, of timing her coffee breaks so she wouldn't run into him in the break room, of taking the long way to her office to bypass his. Two weeks of her heart lurching every time she glimpsed his truck in the parking lot or heard his voice carrying down the hall.

Two weeks of silence.

She supposed they were broken up. What else could she think? He hadn't called. Hadn't texted. Hadn't shown up at her door to talk things through. And she... well, she'd been too hurt, too confused, too everything to reach out either.

At least Cole had been swamped with planning for the camping trip. The three-day, two-night excursion with the athletes had consumed most of his time, giving them both a convenient excuse for the distance between them. She'd heard about it in staff meetings.

She hadn't heard any of it from Cole himself.

Sydney rubbed her temples, willing herself to focus on work. The budget wouldn't analyze itself, and she had a reputation for being thorough, professional, and efficient. She couldn't let her stalled personal life affect her performance.

But the clouds kept drawing her attention, building higher as they spread across the sky like spilled cream.

The memory hit her without warning.

The picnic basket was wicker, she remembered. Cole had borrowed it from the ranch kitchen, promising Chef he'd return it in perfect condition. He'd packed it himself. Sandwiches, fruit, some kind of fancy cheese she'd never heard of, and homemade cookies from the ranch matriarch, Catalina Vargas.

"Scenic overlook," he'd said with a grin that made her stomach flip. "Best view on the whole ranch. Trust me."

And it had been beautiful. They'd spread the blanket on the flat rock outcropping, the valley sprawling below them in shades of gold and rust-red dotted with green palo verde trees. The clouds had been building even then, white and puffy against the brilliant blue sky, but neither of them had thought anything of it.

"In Iowa," she'd said, biting into a strawberry, "clouds like that could mean anything. Thunderstorm, tornado warning, or just another hot, humid day."

"In California," Cole had replied, lying back on the blanket with his hands behind his head, "they usually just mean the marine layer's coming in. Nothing like this."

They'd laughed about their different backgrounds, about the weird weather patterns they'd each grown up with. She'd been telling him about Iowa summers. The oppressive humidity, the corn growing so fast you could almost hear it. That's when the first fat raindrop hit her nose.

"Huh," Cole had said, sitting up. "That's weird."

Then the sky opened up.

Sydney had never seen rain like that. Not the thunderstorms that rolled across Iowa fields, not even the occasional spring deluge. This was a wall of water, sudden and fierce and completely unexpected, drumming against the rock so hard it stung.

"The overhang!" Cole had shouted over the roar, leaving the picnic basket behind. "Come on!"

They'd scrambled for the shallow cave. Really just a deep indent in the rock face about twenty feet away. Cole had tried to use the blanket as cover, holding it over both their heads as they ran, but it had soaked through in seconds, getting heavier and heavier until it was just dead weight dripping water down their backs.

"So much for that idea," he'd gasped, laughing, as they pressed themselves against the dry rock wall.

The picnic basket sat abandoned where they'd left it, filling with water like a miniature bathtub. The sandwich bags bobbed, and an apple slowly escaped over the rim.

"Our food," she'd groaned.

But Cole had been looking out at the valley, and his expression had stolen her breath more than the run through the rain. Wonder. Pure awe.

"Look," he breathed.

The washes. Dry creek beds she'd driven over dozens of times without a second thought were transforming before their eyes. Water rushed down from the mountains, carving channels, filling gullies, turning the dusty valley floor into a network of temporary rivers. It was violent and beautiful and utterly foreign to everything she'd known.

"I've never seen anything like this," she whispered.

Cole had wrapped his arm around her shoulders, both

of them soaked and shivering slightly despite the warm air. "Me neither. California storms give you a warning. This is... this is something else."

They'd stood there for almost half an hour, watching the monsoon rage and then pass, leaving the desert washed clean and smelling fresh. The sun had broken through, turning the raindrops on every surface into diamonds.

"Well," Cole had said finally, surveying their drowned picnic basket with a rueful smile, "that wasn't exactly the romantic afternoon I planned."

But Sydney had kissed him, tasting rain on his lips, feeling his surprised laugh against her mouth. "Are you kidding? This was perfect."

And it had been. Not despite the chaos, but because of it. Because they'd laughed instead of fought, adjusted instead of blamed, and found joy in the unexpected disaster.

Because they'd been together, and that had been enough.

Sydney's throat tightened. She pressed her fingers against her eyes, willing herself not to cry at her desk.

She missed him. Missed him so much it was a physical ache in her rib cage. Missed the way he looked at her as if she were everything. Missed his steady presence, his quiet faith, his terrible jokes and his thoughtful gifts, and the way he remembered every little thing she told him.

The dinner with Luca last week kept playing in her mind, an uncomfortable comparison she couldn't shake. He'd been perfectly nice, perfectly professional. He'd chosen a good restaurant. Upscale Italian place in Peoria. And he'd asked about her work, her interests, and her thoughts about the upcoming tennis season.

But she'd spent most of the evening wishing it was Cole sitting across from her. Wishing for Cole's sincere interest in her spreadsheets and budget projections, even when she knew they bored him, instead of Luca's networking-flavored attention.

Wishing for home instead of... whatever that had been.

She'd caught herself twice starting to tell stories that involved Cole, then awkwardly redirected. Luca hadn't seemed to notice, or if he had, he'd been too polite to comment.

Sydney pulled up her calendar, counting the days. The camping trip started tomorrow. Thursday through Saturday. Cole would be back by the weekend. Maybe she could text him. Ask if they could talk. Not the painful non-conversations they'd been having at staff meetings.

Maybe she could tell him she was sorry for how she'd reacted. That she'd been scared and defensive, and she'd said things she didn't mean. That she understood why he'd been worried, even if she didn't agree with everything he'd said.

Maybe he'd tell her he was sorry, too. That he missed her. Those two weeks of silence had been as miserable for him as they had been for her.

Maybe—

A knock on her door made her jump. Sydney looked up to find Luca standing in her doorway, his expression friendly but purposeful.

"Hey, Sydney. Got a minute?"

Her stomach sank. "Sure. Come in."

He stepped inside and closed the door behind him. The spacious office suddenly felt smaller. More intimate. Sydney straightened in her chair, trying to project professional confidence she didn't quite feel.

"I wanted to follow up on our dinner last week," Luca said, settling into one of her visitor chairs. "I'm looking for someone to travel with me, but I wanted to make it official."

Sydney's hands stilled on her keyboard. "Official?"

"I'm offering you a position. Personal assistant. You'd be traveling with me on the tour. Coordinating everything like you did for Madison. Schedule management, meal planning, travel logistics, all of it." He leaned forward, his expression earnest. "You know what it takes. You're the best in the business at this. After working with the team here during my rehab, I know you'd be perfect."

He named a figure that made Sydney's breath catch. It was nearly twice what she made now. With a salary like that, she could pay off her car early, build her savings, maybe even start thinking about buying a house instead of renting. She wouldn't have to do it forever. Maybe just a few years.

"You'd be based wherever I'm competing," Luca continued, clearly reading her stunned silence as interest. "European tour, Grand Slam, the entire circuit. It's a lot of travel, but you know the life. You're good at it. And you'd be working directly with me."

Something in the way he said that last part made Sydney's skin prickle. She looked at him more carefully. At the way he was leaning toward her, at the warmth in his eyes that went beyond professional courtesy.

Oh.

He wasn't just offering her a job. He was interested. In her.

"Luca, I..." Sydney scrambled for words. "This is very generous. I'm flattered."

"But?" Even though he smiled, she could see the tension around his eyes.

"But I need time to think about it. To pray about it." The words came automatically, the same response she'd given to every major decision since she became a Christian. "This is a big change. Going back to tour life. I'd need to consider—"

"Of course," Luca said quickly. "I'm not asking for an answer today. Take your time. A week? Two weeks? I want you to be sure this is right for you."

Sydney nodded, not trusting herself to speak.

She'd left tour life. Deliberately. Left the constant travel, the hotels, the never having a place to call home.

The memory she usually kept at arm's length surfaced

before she could stop it.

Melbourne. January, three years ago. She'd been courtside at the Australian Open, Madison two sets into a quarterfinal match, when her phone buzzed with a text from her mother.

Dad had an accident. He's okay. Don't worry.

Don't worry. As if a lack of worry could ever follow "accident".

It had taken her four days to get to Iowa. Melbourne to Dubai. Dubai to Chicago. Chicago to Des Moines, delayed twice, rerouted once. She'd spent forty-one hours in transit, watching the hours tick by on her phone, her mother's reassuring texts arriving at intervals intended to comfort her. Somehow they only made the helplessness worse.

He's resting well.

The doctor says the leg will heal cleanly.

Really, sweetheart, there's no need to rush.

By the time she'd walked through her parents' front door, her father was already propped up on the couch watching the evening news, the broken leg in a cast, a cup of her mother's coffee in his hand. He looked surprised to see her. Pleased, but surprised. Like her showing up hadn't been a given.

Her mother had hugged her and said gently, the way she said most things, "We didn't want to pull you away from work, honey."

Sydney had smiled and claimed she was fine. She was just glad he was okay.

She hadn't told either of them she'd cried in the Dubai airport at two in the morning, surrounded by strangers, completely unreachable to the people who mattered most. That she felt the distance not as miles but as failure. Failure to get to the people who matter most to her.

She had gone back to the tour as a different woman. No longer satisfied with the false glory of being a world traveler.

And now Luca was offering her that life again. Only this time, the people she'd be leaving behind weren't just her parents in Iowa.

They were Renata and Solana. Madison. Cole.

People who had become home in a way her childhood house never quite had.

And she'd been happy here. Was happy here, despite the mess with Cole. She loved the ranch, loved the work, loved the people she worked with. She loved watching the sports rehab program grow, loved seeing the difference it made in people's lives.

Sydney loved Arizona monsoons and scenic overlooks, and the way the desert smelled after rain.

She loved Cole.

The thought slammed into her with the force of one of those flash floods, undeniable and overwhelming.

"I appreciate the offer," Sydney finally managed, her voice steadier than she felt. "Really. I'll give it serious thought."

"That's all I ask." Luca stood, extending his hand. She shook it, noting the way he held on just a beat too long. "I think we could do great things together, Sydney."

After he left, Sydney sat frozen at her desk, staring at the closed door.

A job offer. Good money. A chance to return to work she was good at, work that had made her valuable and needed.

But it would mean leaving Vargas Ranch. Leaving the community she'd built here, the life she'd started to create. Leaving the first real home she'd ever had.

Leaving Cole.

Assuming there was still anything to leave. They weren't even together anymore. He hadn't spoken to her in two weeks. Maybe he'd already moved on. Maybe he'd decided she wasn't worth the trouble, that her defensiveness and her fears and her inability to see what he'd been trying to tell her made her too much work.

Maybe she'd already lost him, and staying here would mean watching him eventually fall for someone else. Someone who didn't carry baggage from a nomadic past. Someone who fit into his world without effort.

Someone who wasn't her.

Sydney looked out the window. The rain had started, fat drops splattering against the glass, and the washes in the distance were beginning to run. Not a dramatic monsoon like the one she'd experienced with Cole, but enough to remind her of what they'd had.

What they'd lost.

What she desperately wanted back.

Saturday, she told herself firmly. When Cole got back from the camping trip, she'd reach out. They'd talk. They'd figure out if there was anything left to save.

And then, only then, would she make a decision about Luca's offer.

But even as she thought it, doubt crept in. What if Cole didn't want to talk? What if two weeks of silence meant he'd already made his choice?

What if she'd ruined everything, and there was nothing left to fight for?

The rain fell harder, drumming against the window, and Sydney turned back to her spreadsheet with blurry eyes, trying to focus on numbers that suddenly meant even less than they had before.

7

COLE LOADED THE last of the camping gear into the back of an old school wagon, securing the tarp over the Dutch ovens and cooking equipment. The morning sun already warmed the air, promising a perfect day for the trip. Three days, two nights. Time away from the office. Away from the ranch. Away from the constant, painful awareness of Sydney moving through spaces he occupied.

Two weeks. They'd made it through two awkward, miserable weeks of professional distance and careful avoidance. He'd thrown himself into planning this camping trip with an intensity that probably alarmed Derin.

"You good?" Derin stopped and studied Cole.

"Yeah. Good." Cole forced a smile. "Looking forward to getting out there."

Not entirely a lie. Part of him did want this. Space to breathe. Physical activity. Time with the guys away from the complex emotional landscape of the office, where every corner held a memory of Sydney.

"Carter's riding with you," Derin said, jerking his chin toward where the MLB pitcher stood talking with Marco Rossi, the soccer player who would head home next week. "DeShawn is driving the other UTV. Ross is taking the chuck wagon setup. Adan's got the horses."

Cole nodded, checking his mental list one more time.

Everything accounted for. He'd planned this trip the way he used to structure athlete contract negotiations. Every detail considered, every contingency covered, every variable controlled.

Control. As if controlling the camping trip could somehow make up for the complete lack of control in every other area of his life.

"Hey, Cole!" Carter Wakefield waved, his right arm still in the sling that protected his healing shoulder. The pitcher joined him at the UTV, packed full of gear. "Ready to teach me how to be a real cowboy?"

Cole managed a genuine smile at that. The guy approached everything with the same intensity he'd once brought to his ninety-five-mile-per-hour fastball.

"Pretty sure the actual cowboys will do the teaching," Cole called back. "I'll just try not to embarrass myself."

Carter grinned and climbed into the UTV.

Cole's smile faded as he settled into the driver's seat. He meant it as a joke. But it wasn't, really.

"Shoulder feeling okay?" Cole asked as Carter climbed into the passenger seat.

"Good enough." Carter settled in, adjusting the sling. "Doc cleared me for light activity. Nothing that'll aggravate it."

"Ross has activities planned that'll work around that."

Cole started the engine, watching in his rearview as the small caravan began to form. Derin and Adan on horseback. Marco alongside them, looking far more comfortable in the saddle than Cole would have expected from a soccer player. DeShawn driving the second UTV with Javon riding shotgun, his crutches visible above the side panel. Ross bringing up the rear in the chuck wagon.

They pulled out, heading north toward the stretch of Vargas Ranch land set aside for guest experiences. The property extended for miles, transitioning from desert scrub to rolling hills dotted with mesquite and ironwood trees.

Perfect for the modified roundup experience Cole had designed.

"Thanks for this, man." Carter's voice pulled Cole from his thoughts. "I needed to get away from... everything."

Something in Carter's tone caught Cole's attention. The pitcher stared at the passing landscape, jaw tight, shoulders rigid despite the casual words.

"Rough rehab?" Cole kept his voice neutral, giving Carter space to answer or deflect.

"Rehab's fine. It's—" Carter cut himself off, shaking his head. "Nothing. Just ready for a change of scenery."

Cole let it drop. He knew all about topics a man didn't want to discuss. He'd built an entire life around avoiding one.

They drove in companionable silence for twenty minutes, following the dirt road that wound deeper into ranch property. The landscape shifted around them. More scrub brush. Rockier terrain. Deep, dry washes. The authentic Arizona backcountry that tourists paid premium prices to experience at the guest ranch.

The campsite appeared around a bend. A natural clearing surrounded by palo verde and mesquite, with a seasonal creek running along one edge. Perfect spot for camp. Adan was already there, the horses hobbled and grazing. Ross had pulled the chuck wagon near the fire ring, and Derin began unloading the tents and bedrolls.

"Alright, gentlemen." Derin called out, all business now. CEO mode even in cowboy gear. "Welcome to Vargas Ranch's modified roundup experience. For the next three days, we're living like old-time cowboys. Sleeping under the stars. Cooking over fire. Learning skills that ranchers have used for generations."

Cole climbed out of the UTV, stretching muscles tense from the drive. Marco was already moving toward the tree line, craning his neck like he couldn't take it all in fast enough. DeShawn stood with his arms crossed, head tilted, studying the terrain the way Cole had seen him study film. Javon leaned into his crutches and grinned at nothing in particular.

"We've adapted some things for your injuries," Derin continued. "This isn't boot camp. It's about experiencing ranch culture while your bodies heal. Cole, Adan, Ross, and I will teach you different skills. You'll participate in different activities depending on what your body can handle."

"Roping," Adan announced, stepping forward. "I'll be teaching the basics of calf roping. Anyone who's got full use of both arms and shoulders can join me." He glanced at Carter, DeShawn, and Javon. "Sorry, boys. This one's not for you today."

"I can rope," Javon insisted, gesturing with one crutch. "Just give me a stool. I'll do it sitting down."

Adan laughed. "Alright, running back. We'll see what we can do."

"The rest of us," Ross Braxton said, his Montana drawl marking him as the authentic article in a group of wannabe cowboys, "will be learning Dutch oven cooking and camp skills. My sister Haydon taught me everything I know about cooking over coals. We'll have you making biscuits and stew that'll make you forget about restaurant food."

Carter perked up at that. "I'm in. My wife keeps trying to teach me to cook. Maybe this'll finally stick."

Something flickered across Carter's face when he mentioned his wife. It vanished quickly, but Cole noticed it. The same way he'd learned to read athletes during contract negotiations. Body language never lied.

By mid-morning, the group split into their respective activities. Cole stood in front of a roping dummy with Marco and a somewhat precarious Javon, who'd insisted on participating from a stool that Derin had dragged over.

"Alright, basics first." Adan held up a lariat, the loop already formed and ready. "The rope is your tool. It's an extension of your arm, your intention. You're not throwing it at the calf. You're landing it where the calf is going to be."

Cole had practiced this in the evenings over the last two weeks. Those nights when he couldn't sleep, when the house felt too empty, when checking for a text from Sydney for the fifteenth time in a day made him feel pathetic. He'd come out to the arena and worked with the practice dummy until his arm ached and his mind finally quieted enough for a few hours of restless sleep.

It hadn't made him good at roping. But at least he wasn't completely hopeless.

"Build your loop," Adan demonstrated, the rope spinning smooth and controlled above his head. "You want it big enough to drop over the head and shoulders. Watch the rhythm. Feel the weight."

Marco tried first. The loop wobbled wildly, crashed into the ground three feet short of the dummy.

"Nice try," Adan encouraged. "Cole, you're up."

Cole took the rope, feeling the familiar weight and texture. He'd held this exact lariat dozens of times over the past two weeks. Built the loop. Started the spin.

The rope sailed through the air, and dropped neatly over the dummy's head.

"Well, look at that!" Adan clapped him on the shoulder. "You've been practicing."

"A little." Cole retrieved the rope, avoiding Adan's too-knowing gaze. The former PBR champion had an uncomfortable talent for reading people.

They practiced for another hour. Marco improved rapidly. His natural athleticism translated to the new skill. Javon managed a respectable throw from his seated position, whooping when his loop actually caught the dummy.

"Not bad for a guy who can't stand up," the running back crowed.

Cole felt some of the tension ease from his shoulders. This was good. Physical activity that required focus and coordination but not deep thought. He lost himself in the rope's rhythm, the satisfying thunk when the loop found its target.

"Break time," Adan announced. "Let's see how the camp cooks are doing."

They wandered over to where Ross had set up his Dutch oven station. Carter and DeShawn huddled around three cast-iron pots nestled in coal beds.

"Biscuits," Ross announced proudly, lifting the lid on one pot. Golden-brown tops steamed in the midday air. "And a pretty decent beef stew for lunch. Carter's got a knack for this."

Carter grinned, looking more relaxed than Cole had seen him in weeks. "Turns out I can follow a recipe when someone explains it right."

They ate lunch sitting on logs and rocks around the fire ring. The stew was legitimately good. The biscuits even better. Cole enjoyed the simple pleasure of hot food and good company, the Arizona sun warm on his shoulders, the conversation easy and genuine.

No Sydney to avoid. No office to navigate. No constant reminder of the mess he'd made.

But her absence felt like a missing limb. He kept turning to share observations with someone who wasn't there. Kept thinking that Sydney would love this or he should tell Sydney about something before remembering.

Two weeks of silence. Two weeks of distance at work. Missing her every day. Two weeks of dying by inches.

"You good?" Derin settled onto the log next to him, voice low enough that the others couldn't hear.

"Yeah." The lie came automatically.

"Cole." Just his name. The tone that said Derin wasn't buying it.

"I'm fine. Just..." Cole gestured vaguely at the campsite, the activity, and the whole setup. "This is good. Thanks for suggesting it."

Derin studied him for a long moment, but said nothing

as he finished the last bite of his stew.

The afternoon passed in more skill-building. Adan worked with the roping group on timing and accuracy. Ross taught fire management and introduced them to the finer points of regulating coal temperature for different cooking needs. They set up sleeping areas, organized gear, and prepared for the evening meal.

By the time the sun started its descent toward the horizon, Cole felt the pleasant ache of physical exertion in his shoulders and arms. Not the gym-workout soreness he was used to, but still good. More authentic.

Ross had outdone himself with dinner. Steaks seared in the Dutch oven. Roasted vegetables. More of those biscuits. They ate as the sky turned orange and purple, the temperature dropping as night approached.

"Campfire time," Derin announced when the dishes were cleared and stored. "Grab a seat, gentlemen."

They settled around the fire ring. Someone had added more wood, and flames danced against the darkening sky. Stars emerged overhead in their rural vibrancy, as Derin had called it on their first camping trip years ago.

Cole sat between Marco and Javon, watching the fire. This was the part of the trip he'd been both anticipating and dreading. The part where men who'd spent the day working together started talking about real things. Where guards came down and truth emerged in the safety of darkness and flickering flames.

"Thank you all for coming out here," Derin said, his voice carrying easily in the quiet. "Learning cowboy skills and experiencing an adventure is only part of the plan. Now it's time for honest conversation. For brotherhood. For the vulnerability that strengthens us."

The fire crackled. Someone shifted position. The horses whickered softly in the darkness beyond the circle of light.

"When I first met Cole," Derin continued, and Cole's heart rate kicked up, "it was on a trip just like this. Three days, two nights, out in the middle of nowhere. I was leading a guest experience for the ranch, and Cole was the guest. He gave every task two hundred percent. Never complained. Never backed down from anything hard." Derin's voice warmed. "But more than that, he talked about God like He was his best friend. Made me ask questions I'd been avoiding. We became friends on that trip, and that friendship changed my life."

Cole swallowed hard. He remembered that trip. Remembered being fresh from his divorce, running from the shame, desperate for something real to hold onto. He'd found it in Derin's genuine curiosity, in the honesty that came from working alongside someone under the Arizona sky.

"The point is," Derin said, "sometimes we need to step away from our normal lives to see what's really going on. To say the things that are hard to say. To ask for help or wisdom or just someone to listen."

Silence settled over the group. The fire snapped and popped.

"I'll start," DeShawn said. The quarterback leaned forward, elbows on his knees. "Surgery went good. Rehab's on track. But I'm—" He stopped. Stared at the fire. "What if I come back and I can't throw anymore? Not like before. Two years left on my contract and if I can't—" He cut himself off. "Been throwing a football since I was eight. Don't know how to be anything else."

"You're more than your arm," Ross said.

"Am I?" DeShawn's jaw tightened. "That's all anyone's ever seen. All I've got."

"My family's counting on me," Marco said, his voice low. "Came here from Portugal when I was twelve. Every game I play, every contract I sign—it's not just mine. It's theirs. All of them back home watching. Waiting for me to make it." He shook his head. "What if I let them down?"

Cole stared into the flames. Nobody moved.

"I don't know if I want to come back," Javon said finally. The running back shifted on his log, adjusting the crutches propped beside him. "ACL's healing fine. Doc says I'll be good as new. But maybe—" He stopped. Started again. "Maybe this is God saying I'm done. Maybe I've been holding onto something He's trying to take away."

Cole's throat tightened. These guys were just laying it out there. No pretense. No perfect answers.

He should say something.

The words wouldn't come.

"Carter?" Derin prompted gently. "You've been quiet."

The pitcher stared into the fire for a long moment. His jaw worked as if he were chewing words, trying to decide if they were safe to swallow or needed to be spat out.

"I think my wife is having an affair," Carter said finally, the words flat and toneless. "I don't have proof. Just... a feeling. The way she looks at her phone. How she's always busy when I call. The distance between us started before my injury but got worse after." He laughed, the sound bitter. "We've been married almost five years. And I think she's done with me. We have a daughter, Reed."

The fire crackled in the heavy silence.

"Have you talked to her about it?" Ross asked.

"What do I say?" Carter's voice broke. "'Hey honey, I think you're cheating on me, want to confirm?' She'll either lie or tell me the truth, and I don't know which one terrifies me more."

"The truth is better," Javon said. "Even if it hurts."

"Is it?" Carter looked around the circle, his eyes landing on Cole. "Is truth really better when it destroys everything you thought you had?"

Cole's heart hammered against his ribs. Every eye in the circle had followed Carter's gaze. They were all looking at him now. Waiting for wisdom. For guidance. For the spiritual leadership he'd given Carter years ago when he'd led him to Christ.

He should tell Carter that God could redeem any marriage. That prayer and counseling could fix what was broken. That giving up wasn't an option for believers.

Except Cole knew better. Knew that sometimes marriages ended despite prayer and counseling and good intentions. Knew that divorce wasn't always about giving up. Sometimes it was about accepting that two people couldn't make it work no matter how much they wanted to.

"Cole?" Carter's voice cracked. "You led me to Christ. You told me God had a plan for my life. Does that plan include my marriage falling apart? Does it include becoming a divorced father with split custody and a daughter who grows up thinking Dad couldn't keep their family together?"

The desperation in Carter's voice mirrored the desperation Cole had felt six years ago. The same questions. The same fear. The same shame of failure.

Cole's throat closed. He couldn't breathe. Couldn't think. Every instinct screamed at him to deflect, to give platitudes, to maintain the image of the man who had it all together.

But Carter deserved better. They all did.

"Divorce isn't the end of the world." The words came out rough, barely above a whisper. "I should know. I got divorced six years ago."

The silence that fell over the campfire was absolute. Even the flames seemed to still.

Derin's head whipped toward him, eyes wide with shock. "What?"

"I was married in my early twenties." Cole couldn't look at anyone. Couldn't meet the stares he felt boring into him from every direction. "College sweetheart. We rushed into it. Young. Stupid. Thought love would be enough."

"Cole—" Derin started.

"I was building my career as a sports agent." The words tumbled out now, a dam broken after years of containment. "Traveling constantly. Never home. She needed me, and I chose clients over her every single time. I couldn't prioritize her. Couldn't be the husband she needed. After two years, she left. Divorced me. Married a youth pastor a couple of years later. They have three children now. The perfect Christian family I never gave her."

Carter's face had gone pale. "You never told me."

"I never told anyone." Cole's voice cracked. "Even Sydney doesn't know."

Derin made a strangled sound. "Sydney doesn't—you've been dating her for over a year and you never—"

"I was ashamed." The confession tore out of him. "I failed at marriage. Failed as a Christian husband. How do you tell someone you want to marry them when you've already proved you can't do it? When you've got a divorce certificate and an ex-wife's Instagram full of proof that someone else could give her everything you couldn't?"

"Bro." Adan's voice was gentle. The former bull rider moved closer, placing a hand on Cole's shoulder. "That's a heavy load to carry alone."

"I couldn't—" Cole's breath hitched. "I couldn't tell Sydney because what if she looked at me the way—" He cut himself off.

"The way your ex-wife did?" Ross finished quietly.

Cole nodded, not trusting his voice.

"Cole." Derin's voice was tight. "We're best friends."

"I was a coward." Cole forced himself to look at Derin. Saw the hurt there. The betrayal. "I built my whole life around pretending it never happened. If I don't acknowledge it—" He stopped. "Maybe I thought it would stop being true."

"Except it doesn't work that way," DeShawn said. "Ignoring something doesn't make it disappear."

"No." Cole let out a shaky breath. "It just makes it bigger. Makes it poisonous. I've been carrying this for years and it's ruined everything. I can't propose to Sydney because I'm terrified of failing her the way I failed my ex. I almost did it five times. Had the ring. Had the moment. Choked every single time."

"Five times?" Marco's eyes widened.

"Christmas. Valentine's Day. A trail ride. Random Tuesday at work. Her thirtieth birthday two weeks ago." Cole's hands shook. "That birthday was the final straw. She's done waiting for me to figure out my life. We haven't really talked in two weeks. Just awkward professional interactions at work. I'm losing her."

Carter's eyes were wet in the firelight. "So what do I do? If my marriage is falling apart, what do I do?"

Cole looked at the pitcher. At this man he'd led to Christ. This man, who'd looked up to him, trusted him for spiritual guidance.

"You tell the truth," Cole said. "Even when it scares you. You talk to your wife. Fight for it if there's something to fight for." His voice dropped. "But if it ends—it doesn't make you a failure. Doesn't mean God's done with you. Doesn't mean you can't—" He stopped. "You can still have a future."

"You believe that?" Carter asked.

"Trying to." Cole wiped his face, surprised when his hand came away wet. "Trying to believe the divorce doesn't mean I'm—" He couldn't finish. Started again. "For years I've been sure I don't deserve another shot. That I'm too broken for what I want with Sydney."

"You should have told me," Derin said, voice rough.

"I know."

"But I get it." Derin's gaze dropped to his hands. "I hid stuff from Madison too. Thought I had to be perfect, or she'd leave."

"How did you—" Cole stopped.

"Told her everything. Let her see it all." Derin met his eyes. "She loved me anyway. Sydney deserves that shot, bro. To see who you really are and choose for herself."

"What if she can't get past it? The hiding?"

"Then you tried." Adan's voice was quiet. "Gave her the choice. But not telling her? That's worse than the divorce ever was."

The fire crackled. Nobody moved.

"Thanks," Carter said after a while. His voice was steadier. "Needed to hear that."

"Yeah," Cole said. "Me too."

"This." Ross gestured at the circle. "This is what it's for. Carrying the weight together."

Marco nodded. "Glad you said it. Makes the rest of us feel less—" He didn't finish.

They sat there as the fire burned lower. Talked some. About failure. About trying again. About who God said they were versus who they feared they'd become.

Cole felt lighter. Still raw. But lighter. The thing he'd been carrying for years was out. At least with these guys.

Derin caught his eye across the fire. They needed to talk. About Sydney. About what came next.

But right now, under the stars with men who'd just trusted him with their own broken pieces, Cole could breathe.

First time in two weeks.

8

THE AROMA OF fresh popcorn filled Madison and Derin's living room as Sydney curled into the corner of the leather sectional, a fuzzy throw blanket draped across her lap. Through the floor-to-ceiling windows, the last streaks of sunset painted the desert sky in shades of coral and gold. She loved Arizona evenings like this.

"Your landscape designer did an amazing job with those desert willow trees along the driveway." Sydney accepted the glass of sparkling cider Madison handed her. "And the brittlebush is already blooming. The yellow really pops against all that stone."

"Derin's mom had strong opinions about drought-tolerant plants." Madison settled onto the opposite end of the sectional, tucking her legs beneath her. Her movements seemed slower than usual, more careful. "She practically drew up the entire planting plan herself. But I have to admit, she was right. Everything looks gorgeous, and we barely have to water anything."

Sydney glanced around the open-concept space—soaring ceilings with exposed beams, a stone fireplace that stretched to the roofline, warm wood floors that gleamed in the lamplight. The house was stunning, custom-built to Madison and Derin's specifications over the past year. They'd moved in just a few months ago, and already it looked like a home.

"I still can't get over how much natural light you have in here," Sydney said. "Those windows are incredible."

"Best part of the house." Madison smiled, but didn't reach for her sparkling cider. She'd set it on the coffee table and left it there, untouched. "Derin designed the whole layout to capture the sunrise and sunset views. Though I'm learning that also means every smudge and fingerprint shows up in the morning light."

"The price of beauty."

"Something like that." Madison picked up the popcorn bowl, offering it to Sydney before taking a handful herself. "Though honestly, I'm still learning how to take care of everything. The landscaping, the indoor plants Derin's sister-in-law gave us as a housewarming gift. I killed a succulent last month. A succulent, Syd. Aren't those supposed to be impossible to kill?"

Sydney laughed. "You probably over-watered it. That's usually what gets them."

"See, I need lessons." Madison gestured to the potted plants scattered around the room—a fiddle leaf fig near the window, some kind of trailing vine on the bookshelf, a collection of smaller succulents on the mantel. "I want to be one of those people with a green thumb, but I do not know what I'm doing. Derin just keeps telling me to read the care tags, but that feels like cheating."

"It's not cheating. It's following instructions." Sydney studied the fiddle leaf fig. "That one looks happy, at least. Good light, probably getting the right amount of water."

"Pure luck." Madison made a face. "I've been terrified to touch it in case I mess something up."

"Plants are pretty forgiving if you pay attention to them. Most of them will tell you what they need. Drooping leaves usually mean water, yellow leaves often mean too much water or not enough light." Sydney relaxed into the familiar topic, grateful for something simple to focus on. "The succulents on your mantel probably only need water every couple weeks. The fiddle leaf fig, maybe once a week depending on how dry the soil gets."

Madison leaned forward, genuinely interested. "How do you know all this?"

"My mom." The words came out before Sydney could stop them, surprising her with the lack of accompanying ache. "She had a whole sunroom full of plants. Used to make me help her water them every Saturday morning. I complained about it constantly, but I guess some of it stuck."

"I had no idea." Madison's expression softened. "That's actually really sweet."

Sydney shrugged, uncomfortable with the sentiment. "Anyway, you're doing fine. The fact that most of them are still alive means you're not a complete disaster."

"Low bar, but I'll take it." Madison laughed, then grimaced slightly and set the popcorn aside, her hand drifting to her stomach.

Sydney had been noticing these moments all week. Madison arrived late to the office with vague excuses about sleeping in or stopping by the main house. Turning pale at the smell of breakfast burritos during yesterday's staff meeting. The untouched sparkling cider. The careful, slower movements.

"Mad?" Sydney studied her friend more carefully. "Are you okay? You've seemed a little off this week."

Madison glanced at her. When she spoke her voice sounded both nervous and joyful. "Actually... I wanted to tell you something. That's kind of why I suggested tonight, while the guys are all gone."

Sydney's heart kicked up its rhythm. "What is it?"

"I'm pregnant." The words tumbled out on a breath, and Madison's eyes filled with happy tears. "Almost seven weeks. We weren't trying, but we weren't exactly not trying either, and I took three tests just to be sure, and—" She laughed, pressing her fingers to her lips. "We're having a baby."

"Oh, my!" Sydney launched herself across the sectional cushions, pulling Madison into a fierce hug. "This is amazing! I'm so happy for you!"

Madison hugged her back, laughing and crying at the same time. When they finally pulled apart, she wiped at her cheeks. "We told our families last week, but I wanted to wait until after my first doctor's appointment before making it public. You're the first friend I've told."

Warmth spread through her. "Thank you for telling me. And that explains why you've been sneaking into the office late."

"Morning sickness is real." Madison made a face. "And apparently my body thinks all-day sickness is more accurate. Though it's getting better this week, thank goodness."

They spent the next twenty minutes talking about due dates and doctor appointments, and Madison's plans for juggling work and motherhood. How they'd convert one of the upstairs bedrooms into a nursery. Whether Derin's mom would completely take over baby shower planning. Whether Madison would find out the gender or wait to be surprised.

Sydney listened, asked questions, celebrated each detail, and tried to ignore the small, wistful ache beneath her happiness. She loved Madison was starting this new chapter. Loved seeing her friend glow with excitement and nerves.

But it also highlighted everything she wanted so desperately for herself. Everything she'd been quietly hoping for. Everything she was afraid might never happen if Cole kept holding her at arm's length.

"Okay, enough about me." Madison reached for the popcorn bowl again, managing a few kernels this time. "Your turn. What's going on with you and Cole?"

Sydney's throat tightened. She'd known this was coming—had actually wanted to talk to Madison about everything—but now that the moment was here, the words tangled.

"Syd?" Madison's voice gentled. "You've seemed off this week too. Different."

"We're not together." The words came out flat. "I mean, we haven't officially broken up or anything. But we haven't spoken in a few weeks either. So I guess we're just in limbo."

Madison shifted closer, concern etching lines across her forehead. "What happened?"

"I don't even know." Sydney pulled the blanket tighter around herself. "After my birthday, things just felt wrong. Like we were going through the motions, but neither of us knew how to fix it. And then we just stopped trying. Stopped talking. Started avoiding each other."

"That doesn't sound like you two."

"No." Sydney's vision blurred. "It doesn't."

"Do you want to fix it?"

Did she? Could she?

"I don't know if there's anything left to fix," Sydney admitted. "Maybe he's already moved on. Maybe he's decided I'm not worth the trouble."

"Sydney." Madison's voice carried a note of challenge. "Do you actually believe that?"

Sydney closed her eyes. "I don't know what I believe anymore. I just know that nothing has been the same since my birthday."

"Have you tried talking to him?"

"He's been avoiding me as much as I've been avoiding him." Sydney swiped at her eyes. "But I know I need to. I've been planning to text him when he gets back from the camping trip. Ask if we can talk."

"That's good." Madison squeezed her hand. "That's a start."

"What if he says no? What if he doesn't want to talk? What if the silence means he's already made his choice?"

"Then at least you'll know. But Syd, I've seen the way Cole looks at you. I don't think two weeks changes that."

Sydney wanted to believe her. Desperately wanted to

believe that whatever they'd had was strong enough to survive the distance they'd put between them. But fear kept whispering all the reasons it might not be.

"There's something else." Sydney drew a shaky breath. "Luca offered me a job."

Madison's eyes widened. "A job? What kind of job?"

"Personal assistant. Traveling with him on tour." Sydney's voice came out steadier than she felt. "He said I'm the best at it. That he needs someone who understands how he works."

"Wow." Madison leaned back against the cushions.

"The money's incredible. Nearly double what I make now. I could pay off my car, build real savings, and maybe even buy a house, eventually."

"But it would mean leaving." Madison's gaze held steady on hers. "Leaving the ranch. Leaving Arizona."

"Leaving Cole." Sydney's voice cracked on his name. "Assuming there's even anything left to leave."

They sat in silence for a moment. Sydney's shoulders tensed. It would mean going back to tour life with its constant motion, hotels, and never having roots. The work she was good at, the world she understood. The safety of never staying in one place long enough to get hurt.

Or stay here. At the ranch. In this community. Near Cole. Fighting for something that might already be over.

"What do you want?" Madison's question was quiet.

"I don't know." Her stomach ached. She twisted her hands in her lap. "Part of me wants to take the job. Run away before I can get hurt any worse. Before I have to face the fact that Cole and I are probably done. But the other part..." She trailed off, unable to finish.

"The other part wants to stay."

Sydney nodded, not trusting her voice.

"Then stay." Madison's hand found hers again. "Stay and talk to Cole. Stay and figure out if this can be repaired. Don't run just because you're hurt and disappointed."

"What if I stay and it doesn't work out? What if I turn down this incredible opportunity and then Cole and I can't fix whatever's broken between us?"

"What if you leave and spend the rest of your life wondering what might have been?" Madison countered gently. "You left tour life for a reason. You came here looking for something different. Have you found it?"

Had she? Sydney thought about the past year and a half. Morning coffee with Renata and Solana, the three of them praying together before the day started. The athlete services program she'd built from nothing, watching it become something athletes counted on. Bible study on Thursday nights. A church that finally felt like hers.

Cole's laugh. The way he remembered the little things important to her, even the things she'd only mentioned once. The way he looked at her, like she was precious and he knew it.

The way her heart had come alive again after years of just going through the motions.

"Yes," Sydney whispered. "I found it."

"Then don't walk away from it without a fight." Madison's voice was thick with emotion. "Talk to Cole. Tell him you're scared. Tell him about the job offer. Tell him everything. And then figure out together what comes next."

"What if he doesn't want to talk? What if he's already made up his mind without me?"

"Then you'll deal with that when it happens. But don't make his choice for him, Syd. Don't assume you know what he's thinking or feeling. Give him a chance."

Sydney nodded slowly, letting the words sink in.

"Tomorrow," she said, more to herself than to Madison. "I'll text him when he gets back."

"Good." Madison smiled, reaching for her sparkling cider and taking a tentative sip. "And for what it's worth? I don't think you're going to take that job. I think you already know what you want."

Did she? Sydney wasn't sure. But sitting here in Madison's beautiful new house, celebrating new life and new beginnings, she felt something shift. A loosening of the fear that had been holding her hostage. A tiny spark of hope that maybe she could be brave enough to fight for what she wanted.

"When did you get so wise?" Sydney managed a wobbly smile.

"Pregnancy hormones." Madison grinned. "They're giving me all sorts of insights."

They settled back into the sectional cushions. They talked about plans for Madison's baby shower and funny guest requests from the week. But beneath the easy chatter, Sydney's mind kept circling back to Cole. To the decision waiting for her.

By the time she headed back to her own apartment an hour later, the desert night cool against her skin and stars blazing overhead, Sydney knew she couldn't keep hiding. Couldn't keep pretending the past few weeks hadn't been miserable. Couldn't keep running from the possibility that what she and Cole had was worth fighting for, even if it terrified her.

Tomorrow the guys would come home from camping. And she would text him.

Whatever happened after that... well, maybe that was what faith looked like. Stepping forward even when you couldn't see the path ahead.

COLE ROLLED HIS sleeping bag tight, secured it with the straps, and added it to the pile of gear waiting to be loaded. First light was just breaking over the hills, painting the sky in shades of orange and pink. He'd been awake for an hour already. Maybe longer.

The campsite looked different in the dawn light. Smaller somehow. Less significant. The fire ring was cold ash. The Dutch ovens sat cleaned and stacked near Ross's chuck wagon. The horses grazed quietly in the pre-dawn stillness.

Yesterday had been awkward as anything.

He'd worked alone most of the day. Helped Ross break down the cooking station. Practiced roping with Marco until his shoulder ached. Kept his head down and his eyes off Derin at meals.

Derin had let him. Given him space. But Cole could feel that ending now, in the way his friend packed up the campsite, working steadily closer with each load.

Cole grabbed his duffel and carried it to the UTV. He could be loaded and gone in fifteen minutes. On the trail before anyone else had finished packing.

Coward.

Same word he'd used the other night. Because he was a coward.

"Help me with this?" Derin's voice came from behind him.

Cole turned. His friend stood beside one of the large coolers, the kind that took two people to lift when full. It was empty now. Could've managed it alone easily enough.

But that wasn't the point.

"Yeah." Cole moved to take the other end.

They lifted it together, carried it to the supply area in silence. Set it down.

"We need to talk," Derin said.

"I know."

Derin leaned against one of the UTVs, arms crossed. Not angry. Just waiting.

Cole grabbed another bag from the pile, carried it to the side-by-side, then came back.

Derin hadn't moved.

"I should've told you," Cole said, rubbing a hand on the back of his neck. "Years ago. When we first became friends. I should've—"

"Yeah. You should have."

The bluntness stung. But that was Derin. No cushion, no softening.

"I'm sorry."

"I know you are." Derin pushed off the UTV. "I thought we didn't keep secrets. But I get why you did."

"Do you?"

"I hid things from Madison. Stuff I wasn't proud of." Derin's jaw worked. "Who I was before I started actually living what I claimed to believe. If she'd known, I thought she'd see me differently. See me as someone to walk away from." He shrugged. "So yeah. I get it. Doesn't make it right."

They stood there in the growing light. Around them, camp stirred. Ross emerged from his tent and started hitching the team to the chuck wagon. Carter and the others packed their gear slowly, still half-asleep.

"The other night when you said Sydney doesn't know." Derin shook his head. "Bro, you want to marry her. You've been carrying a ring for six months. And she doesn't know this."

Cole said nothing.

"When were you planning to tell her? After the wedding?"

Still nothing. Because there was no answer. He hadn't been planning to tell her. Or anyone. Ever.

"I don't know how," he said finally. "We've been together for so long. Every conversation we've had about the future while I hid this one thing. She's going to be furious."

"She's going to be justified in that." Derin said. "But she deserves the chance to decide what to do with it. You're making the choice for her."

Cole moved to the next cooler, waited for Derin to take the other end. They carried it in silence before setting it down.

"You need to tell her." Not a suggestion. "Tonight. Soon as we get back. Don't give yourself time to think your way out of it."

"She'll have questions I don't have answers to."

Derin's voice lost some of its edge. "Sydney's tougher than you seem to think. And she loves you. That doesn't mean she won't be angry. But she deserves the truth."

Cole wanted to believe that. "I'll tell her."

"Tonight."

"Tonight."

Derin studied him for a long moment, then nodded. "Good. Now help me load the rest of this gear. I want to be back by lunch."

They worked in silence. The rhythm of packing, loading, securing. Around them, the others did the same. Carter, DeShawn, Javon, and Marco clustered near the UTVs, talking low. Whatever had shifted the other night had changed something between all of them.

"Hey." Derin's voice had settled, less hard now. "You did the right thing the other night. "

"Carter asked me a direct question."

Derin secured the last strap. "Hardest part's done."

Cole glanced at his friend. He'd watched Derin struggle with his own secrets. Seen him confront them head-on. Now he was standing here, married, settled, and whole. Proof that naming it wasn't the end of the world.

Maybe it was a start.

Cole grunted as he hoisted the last bag into position and scanned the campsite. They were almost done.

Ross had the chuck wagon team hitched and ready. Adan was double-checking the fire, his horse already saddled nearby.

"Go to her tonight," Derin said. "Don't plan it to death. Just go."

"I will."

Cole climbed into the side-by-side. Carter dropped into

the passenger seat a moment later, pulling the door shut and settling in like a man who'd slept hard and worked harder.

They rode in silence for a while. Desert scrub rolling past. The sun climbing. Cole kept his eyes on the trail ahead.

"Hey." Carter's voice was easy. Unhurried. He stared out at the passing landscape rather than at Cole. "What you shared the other night. Meant something. To all of us."

Cole kept his hands on the wheel. "Glad it helped."

"Just—yeah." Carter nodded once, like that settled it. "Praying for you, man."

Cole glanced over. Carter was still looking out at the desert, giving him the out of not having to respond to it head-on.

"Praying for you too," Cole said.

Carter stretched his arm out the open window and let it ride the air current, and neither of them said anything else the rest of the drive.

The ranch appeared on the horizon. Home. Except it hadn't felt like home in weeks. Wouldn't, until he stopped carrying this.

He parked and cut the engine. Carter climbed out and grabbed his things, waving farewell.

Cole's phone buzzed with multiple notifications stacking up as the signal returned.

He picked it up. Texts from Madison. A couple from staff members about business. And then, near the bottom—

Sydney's name.

Can we talk? I have something I need to tell you.

Cole stared at it. Relief washed over him. She wanted to talk. She hadn't completely given up on him.

His mind drifted to the early days of their relationship. Three weeks into her job at the sports center. Two dinner dates. Before their DTR conversation. She found him after her shift, cheeks flushed, as if she were steeling herself to say something out loud that she'd rather not admit.

"I called him the wrong name," she'd said, collapsing in

the chair across from him in his office. "Right there at intake. His form was sitting in front of me and I looked up and called him Jamal Duran."

Cole had kept his face straight. "Who?"

"Darnell Johnson!" She pressed both hands over her face. "I called a football player by a basketball player's name. To his face. With his actual name written right there in front of me."

He could still see the color in her cheeks. The way she'd dropped her hands and looked at him, waiting for the verdict. Two dinner dates, and he'd already known he couldn't let her drown in it alone.

"I once called my own client by the wrong name."

She'd blinked. "Your client."

"Marcus Reeve. Spent months on the phone with the man. Knew his voice better than my mother's. Walked into that meeting and called him Maurice." Cole had shaken his head. "To his face. In front of the New York Jets' head coach. At least your slip of the tongue was the first time you met him. I had no excuse."

Sydney had stared at him for a long moment. Then she'd started laughing.

"Your client," she murmured.

Then she calmed. "I guess you're not going to fire me then?"

That look she gave him. It settled somewhere deep in a way he hadn't been ready for.

Looking back now, his moment of vulnerability had opened the door for what came next.

Sydney had sat with him at church the following Sunday. Hadn't missed a single weekend together since.

Until her birthday. When he'd failed her. When he couldn't bring himself to say why.

Cole looked at her text again.

Maybe she was done. Maybe three days completely apart had clarified things for her the way the camping trip had clarified things for him, just in the opposite direction.

Maybe she was still fighting for them. The way she always had.

He pocketed his phone and climbed out of the UTV.

Derin caught his eye across the lot. Raised his chin.

Cole gave him a nod.

He squared his shoulders. He knew what he had to do. Knew it the way he knew the sky overhead was blue.

Doing it was another matter entirely.

9

COLE TURNED HIS key in the front door instead of entering through the garage. He pushed the door open and dropped his camping gear in the foyer.

Then he looked up.

Same boxes. Same bare walls.

She was right.

The tension coiled through his shoulders as he finally saw what Sydney had. A man who paid lip service to his own dreams and goals. A man who hadn't settled into his new life.

No more.

He had said he wanted a quieter life—the Western lifestyle. His version of the cowboy life.

But these unpacked boxes told a different story. They quietly stated the truth which Sydney had read plainly. Cole Gregory wasn't committed to himself, to his life. So how could he ever commit to her.

No more.

He headed straight for the first box across the living room. He didn't eat. Didn't shower off three days of camping grunge. Just started unpacking boxes from the second bedroom, the hall closet, and the garage corner where he'd shoved them the day he moved in.

If Sydney came by—and she might, she'd texted twice

while he was gone and he hadn't known what to say—she wasn't going to find the same packed-up house she'd walked out of two weeks ago.

Instead, she would find books on the shelf. Framed photos on the side table. The good coffee mug in the cabinet.

Cole set the last empty box against the garage wall and came back to lean in the doorway, taking in the room.

Months too late. But done.

The living room looked different without the cardboard. Bigger, somehow. The furniture sat where he'd shoved it ten months ago, oriented toward the television, angled away from the window with its view of the scrubby desert landscape and the distant ridge line turning gold in the late afternoon light.

He'd put it off long enough to make the unpacking feel like penance. Yet, he felt freer. Settled.

His phone buzzed on the kitchen counter.

I'm out front. Can we talk?

Sydney.

Cole closed his eyes. Drew a slow breath through his nose, exhaled through his mouth.

She was here. Now. When every nerve in his body was already worn raw and he smelled like campfire and dust and three days without a proper shower.

He crossed to the front door and opened it before he could talk himself out of it.

She stood on the porch steps, her red hair catching the last of the afternoon sun. She wore jeans and a pale yellow blouse. No makeup, or not much. The freckles across her nose were more visible without it. She held her keys in both hands, turning them slowly, the way she did when she was working up to something difficult.

"Hey." He stepped back from the doorway. "Come in."

She entered, faltering briefly.

He watched her eyes take in the room. The empty shelves with books on them now. The framed print he'd bought in Scottsdale two years ago, finally hung. The throw blanket folded over the arm of the couch.

Her expression shifted, something moving through it too quickly for him to read.

"You unpacked," she said.

"Yeah." He rubbed the back of his neck. "Camping gave me time to think."

She nodded, not quite looking at him. Her hands still worked the keys, one small rotation at a time.

"Can I get you something? Water?"

"I'm okay." She moved to the center of the room and stopped, turning to face him. Her chin lifted slightly. That particular angle meant she'd rehearsed this. Or tried to. "I needed to say some things."

"I know." He pulled out one of the kitchen chairs and offered it to her with a gesture. "Sit down."

She shook her head.

Okay. Standing, then.

Cole leaned against the kitchen doorframe and waited. He crossed his arms, caught himself doing it, and dropped them to his sides. He was braced enough without looking it.

Sydney drew a breath. Let it out slowly.

"I've been hurt," she said. "I want you to understand that before anything else. I'm not angry right now. I was angry. But mostly I've just been—" She pressed her lips together. "Disappointed. And I think you deserve to know what that actually felt like."

The word landed and settled. Disappointed.

"I'm listening," he said.

"I've been patient." She said it without accusation, just fact. "Six months we've talked about marriage, Cole. And I understood, or I tried to understand, that you weren't ready. That you needed more time. I told myself it was worth it. That you were worth it." She paused. "And then my birthday dinner—"

He held very still.

"You looked at me, dropped to one knee, and I thought, this is it, this is finally it." Her voice stayed even. Controlled.

"Then you gave me a necklace. Not a ring. Not after all the conversations about marriage. Not after… You. Dropped. To. One. Knee."

Her hands had stilled around her keys. "Do you know what that felt like? Signaling a proposal and receiving a necklace?"

He didn't answer. Didn't have the right to defend or explain, not yet. She deserved to finish.

"I felt humiliated. Unimportant. Like I'd imagined the entire relationship." Her voice cracked on the last word, just fractionally, and she cleared her throat. "Like maybe I'd been so desperate for what I wanted that I'd convinced myself you felt something you don't actually feel."

"Sydney—"

"I'm not finished." Quiet. Firm.

He closed his mouth.

"And then the things you said afterward." She looked directly at him now, and the steadiness in her eyes was almost harder to hold than anger would have been. "The comment about my biological clock. About how I was feeling pressure from turning thirty." A pause. "I've replayed that a hundred times, Cole. And each time it feels a little worse. Because it wasn't just that you didn't propose. It was that you turned it into something about me. Like my wanting a future together was the problem. Like I was the one creating pressure you couldn't bear."

The words hit him like a fist, steady and deliberate.

She was right. He'd done exactly that. In the scramble to explain himself—to explain nothing at all, really, just to fill the silence where the ring should have gone—he'd said something unforgivable and then wrapped it in enough reasonableness that he'd almost believed it himself.

His throat tightened. The back of his neck prickled with something hot.

"I know," he managed.

"I don't want an apology," she said. "I'm not here for that." The keys settled against her palm. "I want to understand. Because I have loved you. I still love you. But I can't keep waiting for something I don't understand and you won't explain, and I can't keep wondering if the problem is something I've done or something I am." Her voice stayed steady, but he could hear what it cost her. "So I need you to help me understand. If you can."

The room went quiet.

Outside, a mockingbird called from somewhere in the yard, one sharp phrase repeated twice. The refrigerator hummed in the kitchen behind him.

Cole looked at Sydney. At the freckles across her nose, and the careful steadiness of her expression, and the way she was gripping her keys even though she'd said she wasn't angry. At the woman who'd just handed him the most honest accounting of hurt he'd ever been offered and was standing there waiting with more grace than he'd ever deserved.

The familiar response rose in him, practiced and smooth. *It's not you. It's just me. I have some things I'm working through. Give me more time.*

He'd used versions of that for months. Long enough that it probably sounded like the truth.

It wasn't enough. None of it had ever been enough, and he'd spent months patching a wound that needed something else entirely.

But he loved her. Loved her so much. Every day he woke up to an empty space beside him. He wanted her there. As his wife. Knew she wanted it to.

He had to change. So Cole had come home and unpacked boxes. Tried to move into the life he'd been living. Tried to set his mind right before seeing Sydney.

His pulse was loud in his ears. His hands were too still at his sides, as the anxiety climbed up his throat.

He had to tell her the secret he'd kept locked away for years. Long before Vargas Ranch. Long before her. Long before Derin's friendship.

He stifled a snort. For a man who talked to God like a best friend, he'd done a poor job of letting Him anywhere near this particular part of his heart.

And now it would cost him. Maybe everything.

Sydney would finally learn Cole was exactly what he'd been afraid he was. Damaged. Unworthy.

He looked at her again. At the woman standing in his freshly unpacked living room, asking him to trust her with the truth.

She might walk out. She might not.

But she would walk out for certain if he didn't tell her.

He had to tell her about Audrey.

The thought settled over him like the moment before a storm breaks, when the air pressure drops and everything goes still, and he understood, somewhere below thought, that what was coming could not be outrun.

He needed to tell her everything.

"There's something I should have told you a long time ago," he said.

His voice came out steadier than he felt. Which was the one useful thing left over from his former life—knowing how to sound like he had it together even when he absolutely did not.

Sydney's grip on her keys went still.

"I haven't been honest with you." He held her gaze. "Not completely. And before I say anything else, I need you to know that what I kept back wasn't about you. It was—" He stopped. Swallowed. "It's something from before. Something I should have told you from the beginning, and I didn't, and it's the reason I haven't been able to—" He stopped again.

The words tangled in his throat, the same way they always did when the personal stakes climbed past the point where his agent skills could carry him.

He exhaled.

"It's the reason for all of it," he said. "I need to tell you. And I need you to hear me out before you say anything. Can you do that?"

Sydney looked at him. Her expression was unreadable. He noticed the slight tremor in her legs. The signs she was struggling for control.

Then she nodded for him to continue.

———

SYDNEY STEPPED INSIDE and stopped.

The boxes were gone.

She turned slowly, taking in the room she'd stood in two weeks ago with her heart breaking over cardboard and packing tape. Books lined the shelf. A framed print hung above the side table. A throw blanket rested over the couch arm.

He'd done it. He'd actually unpacked.

She'd rehearsed staying steady on the drive over. But standing in a room that finally looked like someone lived in it, the hope came anyway, unbidden and unwelcome.

Maybe this was finally it. Maybe whatever had been holding him back was finally gone.

She turned to find Cole watching her.

And her hope stuttered.

She knew most of his expressions by now. The focused look he wore running athlete schedules. His easy confidence negotiating something he knew he'd win. Even the careful blankness on her birthday, when the night had collapsed around her.

This was none of those.

A shadow moved through his eyes and settled there like something heavy finding its resting place. He looked like a man who had already decided something terrible and was now living in the seconds before it landed.

Her pulse shifted. Her fingers tightened around her keys.

She stood opposite him. Waited.

Cole exhaled slowly. He stood with his hands loose at his sides, his eyes on hers, the effort of holding that eye contact visible in the set of his jaw.

"Before I moved to the ranch," he started. Then stopped. Pressed his lips together. "Before any of this. When I was twenty-two—" He stopped again. Sucked in a loud breath. "I got married."

The word hit her like a physical thing.

Married.

Sydney's grip on her keys tightened.

"Married," she parroted back, the word still not making sense.

"Yes." His voice was low. Too steady. "Her name was Audrey. We met in college. Campus ministry." A pause. "We were young and in love. We thought love was enough."

Audrey?

The name punched straight through her. He'd been married. There had been a wife, a wedding, a whole life he'd never once mentioned.

Her eyes burned. She sank deeper into the chair.

"What happened?" She forced the question out.

"I happened. My career happened." He said it without flinching. "I was building something. Clients, reputation, all of it moving fast. And she was home, waiting. I kept telling myself I'd balance it better next month. Next quarter. After this deal closed." He paused.

"She got frustrated that I wasn't home as much as she wanted." He said it evenly, like a man reciting facts. "I was building my career. Providing everything she needed. Making sure she had—"

His voice trailed off.

Sydney saw it then. The thing Cole had never seen, or had spent years convincing himself he hadn't. His wife—the word drove a knife into her heart—hadn't needed things. She'd needed him. And he'd come home with everything except himself and genuinely believed that was enough.

"She left," he said. "I don't blame her. I gave her every reason to."

Cole rubbed his hand over the back of his neck.

"Divorced me."

The word dropped into the room and stayed there like a silent bomb waiting to explode, destroying everything she longed for. Dreamed of. With him.

Cole's jaw worked. He looked at the floor, then back at her, and for the first time since he'd started speaking he looked less like a man reciting facts and more like a man who'd run out of places to hide.

"I told myself it was ancient history," he said. "That it didn't have anything to do with us. That the man I was back then—the one who couldn't see past his own ambition—wasn't who I was anymore." He stopped. "And then I'd look at you and know I had to tell you. I'd think about how you'd look at me after. I couldn't."

He'd hidden this. Hidden himself. She'd believed he'd let her in…

He'd been carrying this the whole time. She had given him her heart. Had lain awake imagining their future. Had wanted more than she'd wanted anything in years to become his wife.

And he hadn't even told her who he was.

The tears came without warning. Not graceful. Not slow tracks.

She pressed the back of her hand hard against her mouth to stifle the sob ripping through her.

Cole took a step toward her.

"Don't." The word came out broken.

He stopped.

Sydney turned toward the window, toward the desert going gold in the fading light, and tried to breathe through the searing pain.

He'd been married. To someone named Audrey. Every conversation on his porch. Every Sunday sitting beside him in church.

Cole was a stranger. She didn't know him at all.

Her birthday dinner stuck in her memory. How she'd steadied herself walking in that night. How she'd prayed in the car. The way her heart had lifted when he'd reached into his pocket. The way it had shattered when it wasn't a ring.

And the whole time. The whole time he'd been carrying *this*.

Christmas. She'd noticed him go quiet at the ranch Christmas party, a stillness in him she'd attributed to the moment being romantic. Valentine's Day, when he'd reached for something in his jacket pocket and then pulled his hand back empty. The trail ride to the overlook in the spring. That random Tuesday in his office when he'd started to say something, then stopped, then said never mind. She'd replayed each of those moments a hundred times, trying to understand what kept stopping him.

Now she knew.

"How could you?" Her voice shook. "Fourteen months we've been together. I told you things I've never told anyone. About the tour, about being lonely for years, about what it meant to finally have a home." Her throat closed. She pressed her hand harder against her mouth and fought for control she would not find. "I thought you knew me. I thought I knew you."

"I'm sorry." His voice was rough. "I know that's not—"

"You let me think it was me." The words tore out of her. "Every time you didn't propose. Every time you pulled back. I lay awake wondering what was wrong with me. What I wasn't giving you. Why I wasn't enough." She broke off. A sob climbed her throat, and she swallowed it down hard. "And this whole time it wasn't me at all."

She turned to face him. Her face was wet, tears dripping down her chin now. She didn't care.

"I built my whole life here." Her voice cracked on every word. She kept going anyway. "I gave up my life. I planted myself in this place. I built friendships and a church home, and I thought, I genuinely believed, that God brought me here." She stopped. Drew a shaking breath. "I thought you were the reason."

She'd built a life on that belief. Not just a relationship—a life. She'd found her first real home here, her first real community, her first real sense of belonging after years of never having it. She hadn't stumbled into Vargas Ranch. She'd chosen to stay. Had chosen to root herself here, to build friendships and a church family and a role she'd created from nothing, because everything in her had said this is the place.

And she'd believed—she had genuinely believed—that Cole was part of why God had brought her here.

What did it mean if she'd been wrong about that?

The question opened like a crack beneath her feet, and she couldn't look at it straight on. Not yet. Not here.

Cole's face had gone ashen, features twisted in visible pain.

"We talked about marriage." Her voice dropped. "We did. We talked about the future. About kids. About what we wanted *our* life to look like." The sob she'd been swallowing broke through, just once, before she caught it. "And you sat across from me in every single one of those conversations knowing you'd already been married. Already been divorced. And you never said a word."

She sniffed, going quiet, the ache unbearable.

"I know." His voice was barely audible. "I've never been enough. Not for her."

He scuffed his foot on the tile, shifting his weight.

"Not for you."

Sydney's head snapped toward him now, ire rising. "That's not true. If you would have shared who you really were..."

Cole looked away, his shoulders drooping.

Her thoughts shifted, wondering who else had lied to her about Cole. Madison? Derin?

"Who else knows?"

He was quiet one beat too long.

"Who else, Cole?"

"No one." His jaw tightened. "Not Derin. Not anyone. Until yesterday."

Not Derin. His best friend of six years. The man who had trusted Cole with the most devastating parts of his own story and received what? A version of Cole that was carefully, deliberately incomplete.

Not anyone.

The room tilted.

She had loved this man. Still did, and that was the worst part, that was the thing she couldn't outrun standing here in his living room with her face wet and her hands shaking. She loved him. She had been so sure he was it, the one God had placed in her path when she'd finally settled down, finally found a place to belong. She had pictured their life together. A house. Children who would grow up on this land with the mountains in the distance and faith woven into the fabric of everything.

She had been *certain*.

And she hadn't known him at all.

"We're done." The words came out quiet. Not steady. Nothing in her was steady. But clear. "You lied to me our entire relationship." She picked up her keys. Her hands trembled. "I loved you. I wanted to marry you. And I didn't even know who you were."

"Sydney—"

She walked to the door.

Not because she felt strong. Because staying one more

second would break something in her that couldn't be fixed. The evening air rushed in, warm and desert-dry, carrying the faint, clean scent of scrub brush.

She stepped through.

Behind her, the door swung shut with a soft, definitive click.

The path to her car blurred. The mountains had gone purple in the fading light, and the world continued being itself with a completeness that felt almost unbearable.

She got in. Sat with her keys in her lap.

Sydney pressed her forehead to the steering wheel. One long moment, just breathing.

She still loved him. That hadn't changed in the last ten minutes. It probably wouldn't for a long time. If ever.

She didn't know what she was supposed to do with that. With loving someone she didn't know. With the possibility that everything she'd understood about the last fourteen months had a different explanation than the one she'd been living with. She'd been so sure she was the problem. And she hadn't been. And somehow that was almost worse—because it meant the thing standing between them had never been hers to fix.

She had no idea what came next. Where she went from here.

She straightened. Started the car and pulled out.

She didn't look back at the house or at Cole.

10

SYDNEY TOOK THE long way to the conference room.

She didn't decide to. Her feet just went left at the main corridor instead of right, carrying her down the back hallway, through the break room, and around to the conference room the long way. Adding maybe three minutes to a walk that should have taken one. Avoiding the stretch of corridor that ran past the door with Cole Gregory, COO stenciled in clean black letters on frosted glass.

She hadn't done that once. Until now.

She told herself that the longer route was fine. Practical, even. She needed to check whether the break room coffee was fresh before the meeting.

It wasn't. She poured a cup anyway.

The Monday morning operations meeting was already half assembled when she slid into her usual chair at the far end of the table. Ryan and Hudson were going back and forth about scheduling for the incoming collegiate volleyball group. Adan sat across from her, notepad open, something about the men's Bible study this week and God's timing. Sydney caught maybe every third word.

Madison slipped in a few minutes late, cheeks flushed, and exchanged a glance with Derin before taking her seat. She mentioned a doctor's appointment on Thursday and asked to reschedule a mentoring session with one female athlete. Sydney made a note.

She opened her laptop. Pulled up her notes from last week's athlete intake reports. Fixed her eyes on the screen and kept them there.

The meeting moved the way Monday meetings always moved. Agenda items checked off one by one. Madison's scheduling conflict resolved. A catering question for the upcoming guest weekend. Sydney answered when addressed. Luca Marchetti checking out this morning, confirmed. The incoming collegiate volleyball group's arrival time, confirmed. The updated welcome packet would be waiting for them in the Flagstaff six-room casita.

Professional. Competent. Fine.

She didn't look at the door.

"Sydney." Madison's voice came quietly, close, and Sydney realized the room had mostly emptied. She'd been staring at a note on her screen she'd already read three times without retaining it. "Hey."

Madison stood at her elbow. Her blond hair pulled back, concern written plainly across her face.

"I'm good." Sydney blinked rapidly.

"You're not."

Sydney looked at the empty doorway.

"Come on. Let's get a coffee," Madison said, snapping Sydney's laptop closed.

The hallway was quiet.

Madison fell into step beside her without a word, matching Sydney's pace down the corridor, past the break room, and outside. The heat pressed in as they ambled along the path to the dining hall.

Drake Vargas stood behind the counter, working the espresso machine. He glanced up, reading her mood, and asked, "The usual?"

"Please," Madison said.

Sydney nodded.

He turned back to the machine without another word.

They took their cups out to the patio. Empty at this hour. No guest was going to brave the morning once the sun crested Dalton Peak. Heat soaked into the concrete deck. Madison steered them toward a shaded table as the misters clicked on, a quiet exhale of cool mist drifting across the ironwork. Drake, probably. Thinking ahead, the way he always did.

Sydney sat. Pressed her palms flat against the iron table. Stared at nothing in particular.

The tears she'd been holding back since she poured that stale break room coffee crept up without warning. She blinked hard. Swallowed. Blinked again.

Madison sat across from her and said nothing.

"I'm fine," she managed.

"Okay," Madison said, in the tone that meant she'd wait as long as it took.

Sydney tipped her head back. Drew a breath through her nose. The air smelled like dust and something faintly sweet—the flowering scrub along the patio edge. The mountains stood cast in shades of gold and rust. Immovable in the distance, indifferent as always.

She lowered her head.

"We broke up. Cole and I. Saturday night."

Madison was quiet for a beat. "Oh, Syd."

"He had a wife."

Her gaze landed on Madison's face.

"A wife. He was married before. Divorced, years ago, before he ever came to the ranch. And he never told me. Not once."

Madison exhaled slowly, reaching for her decaf latte.

"He wasn't who I thought he was." Sydney set the cup down. "We talked about our future. About kids. About what kind of house we'd want, whether we'd stay in Forepaugh or build nearby. I told him things I had told no one else. And he sat there, every single time, knowing he had this massive secret."

"Derin was as shocked as you are." Madison's voice was careful. Measured in a way that meant she was choosing every word. "He learned about it only on the camping trip."

Sydney frowned.

"Cole told the group at the campfire." Madison met her gaze. "Derin called me Friday night. He was—" She stopped. "He didn't know, Sydney. He had no idea."

Sydney absorbed that. She'd turned it over and over through the long night. Wondering if Derin had known and kept Cole's secret. Hoping Madison hadn't hidden it from her.

Sydney pressed two fingers against the bridge of her nose.

"I keep thinking," she said, "about all the times I thought something was wrong with me. That there was something I wasn't doing right. Something I wasn't giving him." She stopped. "And the whole time—"

"It wasn't you." Madison's voice was firm. No hesitation.

"I know that now." Sydney dropped her hand. "It doesn't make it any better."

The tears trickled down her cheeks, and she looked away. "Despite it all, I still love him."

Madison reached across the table and covered Sydney's hand with hers. Said nothing.

Then Madison withdrew her hand. Sydney wiped her eyes with a napkin.

"But I don't think love is enough. I don't think I can marry a man who hid such a huge part of himself from me. For so long."

Madison nodded slowly. "I get it."

Finally, Sydney stood, smoothing her dress. "We should head back."

She had a volleyball group arriving Thursday and an outgoing athlete to check out this morning, regardless of what had happened. The ranch and sports complex kept moving. So would she.

Madison studied her for a moment with a quiet, careful look. "Call me tonight. Or come over."

"I will." Sydney meant it.

The walk back was quiet, too.

Sydney settled behind her desk, pulled up the checkout queue, and got to work. One task at a time. That was how you got through a Monday.

Half-past nine, her office door opened. Luca Marchetti stood with his travel bag already over one shoulder, unhurried as ever.

He took one look at her and stopped.

"Sydney." The warmth in his voice shifted into something more careful. "You look like—how do you say it—something the cat dragged in."

"Good morning, Luca."

"No, no. I mean this with great concern, not insult." He set his bag down and leaned against the doorframe, studying her. "What happened?"

She pulled up his departure paperwork. "Your transport is confirmed for ten-fifteen. I can have someone bring your remaining luggage from the casita—"

"Sydney."

She stopped.

He pushed off the doorframe and dropped into the chair across from her.

"He wasn't who I thought," she said finally. "Too many secrets."

Luca was quiet for a moment. "Your boyfriend. Cole?"

"We're done."

He didn't rush to fill the silence, which she appreciated. Some people heard news like that and scrambled to cover it with words. Luca just absorbed it, giving it a respectful beat of space.

"I'm sorry."

"It's fine." She pulled his checkout receipt from the

printer and slid it across her desk.

He took the receipt without looking at it. "You know," he said, his tone shifting just slightly, "the offer still stands. The position. The tour." He paused. "I think Europe would be good for you."

Sydney looked him in the eyes. "Luca—"

"I've watched you for six weeks run one of the best athlete services programs anywhere. I need someone exactly like you on the tour. Besides," he offered a slight smile, "a change of scenery might help."

She twisted her hands in her lap. He made a fair point. But she wasn't ready to leave. Vargas Ranch had become her home.

After a beat, he shrugged. "I am flying to London in two weeks. The offer is open until then. No pressure."

"Thank you, Luca. I'll think about it."

He picked up his bag. "Take care of yourself, Sydney."

"Safe travels."

She watched him cross the lobby toward the main entrance, his casual stride the same leaving as it had been arriving, a man entirely at ease in the world he moved through. The glass door swung shut behind him.

The lobby was quiet.

Sydney stood in the lobby for a moment, not moving, looking at the space where he'd been.

Six weeks on the tennis circuit meant London. Paris. Then eventually back to the States. New York City for the US Open in September. A tour she knew well. A role she'd succeeded in before.

Not the life she had dreamed of. At Vargas Ranch. At the sports complex. As Cole's wife.

She thought about the long way to the conference room that morning. The careful rerouting. How long she could keep taking four-minute detours around a door she'd once walked past twice a day without thinking.

Maybe Luca was right.

The thought arrived quietly, without fanfare.

Maybe she should go.

COLE MADE IT to the office on autopilot.

He'd lain awake for hours, staring at the ceiling in a house that still didn't feel like a home, despite finally unpacking. The emptiness clawed at his gut.

As he flipped on the breakroom lights and started a pot of coffee, exhaustion washed over him.

They were over. Done. She'd broken up with him. He'd finally told her the truth about Audrey. About his life.

And she'd walked away, anyway.

He missed his morning routine with Sydney. Could barely remember how their morning Bible and prayer time had started.

Sydney had come in early. He didn't know why. Something she needed to finish before the day started. His office door had been open. He'd heard her footsteps slow in the hallway.

Then he looked up.

She stood in the doorway, one hand on the frame, taking in the open Bible on his desk, the notepad beside it, the cold coffee he'd forgotten to drink. He remembered her expression shifting—not embarrassed exactly, more like she'd walked into something private and hoped she hadn't disturbed him.

"Sorry, I didn't know anyone was here."

"I'm here most mornings." He'd left his finger on the verse he had been reading. "You're welcome to stay."

She'd hesitated just long enough that he'd thought she would go. Then she settled into the chair across the desk from him. He told her what he was reading. She opened her phone to her Bible app and found her place, reading the next verse aloud.

They'd sat like that for twenty minutes. No agenda. No performance. Just two people starting the day the same way, reflecting on Scripture together.

Then she'd come back the next morning. And the one after that.

They began praying together, too. For the staff. The athletes. Each other.

He'd gotten used to reading Scripture aloud, their voices alternating with each paragraph. Nearly a year of mornings that started the same way, in the same quiet, with the same person.

It had ended the day after her thirtieth birthday and his fifth failed proposal.

He stood at the coffeemaker and didn't move for a moment. That sacred time in his office every morning—her voice and his, trading verses back and forth—he'd told himself it was a good habit. Something healthy. Something right.

But he knew what it had really been. A rehearsal for every morning for the rest of his life, in a home that was theirs, with a woman who loved God the way she loved people, without reservation. A wife. His wife.

He'd had the closest thing to it. Every single morning for nearly a year.

The coffeemaker sputtered as the brew filled the pot. He poured one cup. Not two.

Then he scuffed back to his empty, dark office to begin his day.

By noon, Cole had completed dozens of tasks he could barely recall. Routine. Productive. Exactly what Monday looked like from the outside.

The outside was doing fine.

He ate lunch at his desk. A protein bar and the remnants of a bag of stale almonds from his bottom drawer.

At two-fifteen he had to walk past her office.

The door was closed.

He kept walking. Didn't slow down, didn't speed up. She used to keep it open. Her voice spilling into the hallway, phone conversations about work, the occasional burst of laughter at something a guest had said.

He took the long route back to his desk.

At three-thirty, his phone buzzed.

You okay? Derin.

Cole set the phone face down on his desk and returned to the spreadsheet on his screen. He'd deal with Derin later. Or not. Derin knew everything now. Had known since the campfire, since Carter's honest unraveling had pulled the truth out of Cole like a splinter finally worked loose.

Cole hadn't made it easy on his best friend. Hadn't been fair to him. Hadn't been fair to Sydney.

The report blurred.

He blinked and refocused. The financials needed his full attention. He had a budget to approve.

He worked until five-fifteen, which was later than usual but not unusual enough to raise any flags, and then he locked his office and walked through the building alone. The staff had cleared out. The gym was quiet. He pushed through the east exit door into the late afternoon heat. Summer was almost here.

His car sat where he'd parked it at six-forty-seven that morning. The McLaren gleamed under the last of the afternoon sun, orange light running across the hood like something from one of those car ads he'd never thought about until Derin started ribbing him about it.

He drove home.

The house looked the same as he'd left it.

He stood in the doorway for a long moment after stepping inside.

Saturday evening, before Sydney arrived, he'd unpacked everything. Every box. Every surface. The kitchen counter had a fruit bowl, which was aspirational since there was no fruit in the house. He'd plugged in the floor lamp in the living room. Small things. Proving he actually lived here.

He'd unpacked it all as a gesture. Evidence. Confirmation that he was choosing this life, choosing permanence, choosing her. He'd lined up the book spines on the shelf, hoping she would see it.

Sydney had walked in, and he'd told her the truth, and she'd walked back out.

The fruit bowl sat empty on the counter.

He set his keys on the hook by the door and walked to the kitchen. Got a glass of water. Stood at the window that looked out over the perfectly manicured lawn. His landscaper had come by that morning.

Cole drank the water.

He couldn't believe it was over. He still loved her. Wouldn't stop loving her. Ever.

He rinsed the glass and set it in the drying rack.

He should eat. There was nothing in the refrigerator worth calling dinner, but he could order something. Drive into town. Do any number of things that a functioning man did at the end of a Monday.

Instead, he entered the living room and sat down on the couch. The throw blanket was there. He'd picked it up at that home goods store in Wickenburg, the one Sydney had pointed at once from the car window and said something about good throw blankets. He'd gone back two days later.

Cole hadn't told her that.

He hadn't told her many things. That was the problem. That had always been the problem, dressed up in a hundred different reasons.

His phone sat in his pocket. Right as he pulled it out, an Insta notification popped up.

Audrey.

He frowned at it so long that the screen faded to black.

His reflection appeared muted in the dark screen. Tired eyes.

Running a hand through his hair, he closed his eyes on

the edge of a wordless prayer. One breath. Two.

He knew what he must do.

After unlocking his phone, he tapped and swiped. Found her profile. Unfollowed. Done.

Then he opened his contacts. Scrolled past Derin's name. Past Carter, who had his own wreckage to manage. Past the ranch numbers and the vendor contacts and a half-dozen people he'd called in the last week about things that did not matter at all.

He stopped on the name he'd added months ago. The pastor at their church. He'd gotten it from the church website when some vague, theoretical future version of himself had thought he should call him. He'd never called.

Cole stared at the name. A pastor. A spiritual advisor. Maybe a counselor.

His thumb hovered over the name. Making the call meant saying the words out loud to yet another person. Admitting he needed help. Admitting he'd stumbled into such murky waters he couldn't pull himself out.

He called.

The line rang twice and kicked to voicemail. The pastor's voice, familiar from Sunday mornings, was steady and welcoming.

Cole waited for the tone.

"This is Cole Gregory. I attend our church. I'd like to schedule—uh... some counseling appointments if you have availability." A pause. "I should've called a long time ago."

He ended the call and set the phone on the cushion beside him.

Outside, long shadows fell across the yard as the sun dropped. The desert cooled. The house remained quiet.

He didn't feel better. He hadn't expected to. But for the first time in years, he'd asked for help instead of burying the thing deeper and hoping the weight of it would eventually stop being so heavy.

It was a start. A small, insufficient start.

Cole leaned back against the couch and looked at the books on the shelf, their spines aligned, patient, going nowhere.

The house waited around him.

He let it.

11

SYDNEY MADE THE call from her office with the door closed.

A week of closed doors. A week of the long route past the break room, the careful timing of hallway crossings, the deliberate focus on her screen whenever footsteps slowed near her office. A week of holding herself together with both hands.

She couldn't do another one.

Luca picked up on the second ring. "Sydney."

"I'd like to accept the position." No preamble. She'd learned long ago that hesitation only made hard things harder.

A beat of silence, then warmth filled his voice. "I'm very glad to hear it."

He walked her through the details, including the contract his manager would send, the start date, and the London flat already arranged for staff. Two weeks from Friday. She pulled up her calendar and confirmed. He mentioned the first tournament, the travel schedule through August, and the US Open in New York come September. She noted each item, her stylus moving in clean lines across the tablet.

Professional. Organized. Fine.

"Sydney." His tone shifted slightly. "You are sure?"

Her stylus stilled.

Outside her window, the Arizona summer pressed hard against the glass. A pair of athletes crossed the courtyard toward the training facility, water bottles in hand. The sports complex hummed around her, familiar as breathing. The schedule she'd built, the systems she'd created, and the job she'd created from nothing.

"Yes," she said. "I'm sure."

They wrapped up the call in a few minutes. She set her phone face down on the desk and looked at her tablet. Start date. Flight details. Contract pending.

She'd done the right thing. She believed that.

Still, her stomach tightened, and her shoulders dropped.

Shaking it off, she stood and smoothed her skirt. She had drafted the resignation letter this morning in the quiet hour before anyone else arrived. The words had come out steadier than she expected. She printed it now. Signed it. Folded it once. Held it for a moment before sliding it into her tablet case.

The hallway outside her door would take her left, past the break room, past the conference room, and around the long way to almost anywhere on this floor. She'd learned every alternate route in the last week, trying to avoid one specific door.

Cole Gregory, COO. Frosted glass. Clean black letters.

She turned right.

The corridor stretched ahead of her, quiet in the mid-morning lull between meetings. Her heels clicked softly on the tile floor. She kept her chin level and her breathing even. She straightened her shoulders.

Sydney knew exactly what his face was going to do when she walked in. She'd watched that face for more than a year. She knew the careful way Cole held himself when something hurt him, the almost imperceptible tightening around his eyes, and the way the warmth drained out of his expression when he was trying to keep something locked down.

She wasn't ready for it.

She kept walking anyway, the letter feeling heavier with each step.

PASTOR JARED HAD a whiteboard in his office.

Cole had noticed it during their one session four days ago now, Thursday evening, the building quiet after the midweek youth service cleared out. The whiteboard was covered in half-erased diagrams, the remnants of some Bible study lesson, and Cole had stared at it for the first ten minutes while he tried to find the words.

He'd found them eventually.

All of them. The entire story. Audrey, the marriage, the divorce, the shame he'd packed up and carried from California to every city his career had taken him, and finally here, to a house in Forepaugh with an empty fruit bowl on the counter and a woman he'd never deserved. He'd told Pastor Jared everything, haltingly, without the careful editing he'd applied to every version of himself he'd ever displayed to anyone else.

Pastor Jared had listened without flinching. Asked two questions. Prayed with him at the end.

Cole had driven home feeling scraped clean. Not healed. Not fixed. But like a man who'd finally set something down after carrying it so long he'd forgotten what his hands felt like empty.

He'd been trying to figure out what to do with that feeling ever since.

A knock at his open office door pulled him back. Ryan stepped in, tablet in hand, running through the updated rehab schedule for the incoming collegiate group. Cole focused, answered the questions that needed answering, and approved the schedule change for the pool therapy slot on

Wednesday. Standard morning business. Ryan was efficient, and Cole was grateful for it.

"That everything?" Cole said.

"That's everything." Ryan tucked his tablet under his arm and turned toward the door, nearly stepping into Sydney.

"Oh—hey, Syd." Ryan's voice lifted with its usual ease. "Good morning."

Cole's eyes snapped to the doorway.

Sydney stood just inside the frame. Her red hair was pulled back, as it often was at work, neat and professional. She had her tablet case in one hand, held against her side. She wore the careful composure he'd learned meant the opposite of fine.

"Good morning," she said to Ryan.

Ryan slipped past her into the hallway. His footsteps faded.

The office went quiet.

Cole stood, his pulse spiking before his brain caught up.

He didn't know why he stood. Some reflex, some courtesy. Sydney stepped fully into the room, and the door stayed open behind her, morning light falling across the floor between them. She didn't sit. Neither did he.

Her eyes met his for just a moment before dropping to her tablet case. She unzipped the front pocket and withdrew a folded piece of paper.

His stomach dropped through the floor.

She crossed to his desk and set it on the surface between them. One sheet, folded once.

"I've accepted a position with Luca Marchetti's tour." Her voice was even. "This is my two weeks' notice."

The words arrived in the right order. He stood there, understanding them, while something in the center of his chest came apart with a quietness that felt worse than noise.

"Sydney."

She lifted her gaze.

"Is this because of me?"

Something crossed her face. Not anger. Something older and more tired than anger. She held his eyes for three seconds, maybe four, and didn't answer.

She didn't need to.

"I'll ensure a smooth handover," she said. "I can document everything before I go. The intake process, the athletes' files, the scheduling templates. Whoever takes over the role will have everything they need."

Of course she would. Of course, she'd already thought through the transition, the documentation, and even the person who came after her. She'd built this program from nothing, and she would hand it off gracefully and competently before she walked out the door, because that was Sydney Steele.

Cole couldn't speak.

"I'll copy you on the transition notes as I complete them." She picked up her tablet case. "Unless you'd prefer I send them to Derin or Madison."

"No." His voice came out lower than he intended. "Send them to me."

She nodded. One small, professional nod.

She turned toward the door.

"Please close the door on your way out."

She paused. Just for a beat, with her hand on the knob. Then the door clicked shut behind her.

Cole stood behind his desk and looked at the folded piece of paper.

He should pick it up. File it. Forward it to HR. There was a process for this. He knew the process. He'd overseen the process a dozen times in his career, and he knew exactly what happened next.

Instead, he collapsed into his chair as if his legs could no longer hold up his weight.

The office held its silence around him. Outside, the ranch carried on—he could hear the faint sounds of the training facility through the walls. A door somewhere down the corridor. The ordinary hum of a Monday morning moving forward without him.

He pressed the heels of his hands against his eyes.

He had sat in Pastor Jared's office four days ago and said the truest things he'd ever said out loud to another human being. He had come home feeling like a man who was finally ready to start. Like something had shifted, or was shifting, or could shift, given enough time and honesty, and grace.

His hands dropped to the desk. His vision blurred. He didn't blink it clear.

Somewhere in his beard, the tears went quietly, without a witness.

He sat with it for a long time. The resignation letter. The empty doorway. The particular silence of an office where someone's voice used to read scripture with him every morning.

Then he bowed his head.

He didn't ask for her back. Cole already knew better than to pray for what he wanted rather than what was right. He'd learned that much, at least.

He prayed for her.

For the tour, the travel, her new role. For London and whatever came after. For the women's housing room she'd pack up, the roommates who would miss her, the church seat next to him that would sit empty on Sunday mornings. For the life she was walking toward, one that had nothing of him in it, and for the God who would go with her anyway—who would go before her, the way He always had, into every city and season and morning she hadn't reached yet.

Cole lifted his head.

The resignation letter sat on his desk.

He reached for his phone and texted Pastor Jared.

Can we meet again this week?

The reply came back in under a minute.

Thursday. Same time. I'll be here.

Cole set the phone down and picked up the resignation letter. He read it once, folded it again, and did what came next.

It was all he had left to do.

THE HARSH, LOUD rip of the tape gun sent a shiver down Sydney's spine. Solana pressed the strip flat against the top of the last box, smoothed it twice, and set the gun on the windowsill without a word.

That was how the morning had gone. Sydney handing things over. Renata folding. Solana wrapping, sealing, and stacking. The three of them packed the room as if they'd done this before, even though they hadn't—even though Sydney had hoped when they did she'd be moving into a house. With her husband.

Not halfway around the world.

"I think that's everything." Sydney turned in a slow circle.

The room looked wrong. Not empty exactly—the furniture stayed, the bedding, the curtain panels Renata had helped her pick out at the market in Wickenburg last summer. But the things that made it *hers* were gone. The row of books on the low shelf. The framed photo from Renata's birthday hike. The small clay pot she'd found at a craft fair in Prescott and brought home.

She'd packed those things without thinking.

This was the first place she had ever lived that felt like home.

Not a hotel room. Not her childhood bedroom. Not the rotation of temporary accommodations near whatever tournament Madison played that month. *This.* This room, with its two windows that caught the morning light, and this shared space where she had learned slowly and imperfectly what it meant to belong somewhere.

Her throat tightened.

"I left the throw blanket," she said. "The blue one. You can have it, Renata."

Renata looked at the folded blanket on the edge of the bed. "Sydney."

"It's yours. I'll just have to buy another one in London and it won't be the same anyway, so—"

"Stop." Renata whispered it without apology. She crossed the room and took Sydney's hands, both of them. Her grip was warm and steady. "Look at me."

Sydney looked.

"You built a home here." Renata's voice was quiet but clear. "A rich, fulfilling life. Not just a job, not just a place to sleep. You put down roots in this room, in this ranch, with us. And those roots are still there whether you stay or go. But I need to ask you something, and I need you to answer me honestly."

Sydney's throat closed up. "Renata—"

"Do you want to leave?"

Sydney hadn't expected that. She opened her mouth. Closed it.

Solana didn't look up from the box she was lifting to stack against the wall, but her hands stilled for just a moment.

"The job is good," Sydney said finally. "The salary is—"

"That's not what I asked you."

The morning light came through the window at an angle that touched the curtain panels and spread gold across the floor between them. Sydney had watched that light a hundred times. She'd prayed in it, cried in it, and drunk her coffee in it on slow weekend mornings when the ranch was quiet and she felt, for the first time in her adult life, like she didn't have anywhere she needed to rush to.

"No." Her voice came out smaller than she meant it to. "I don't want to leave."

Renata squeezed her hands. "Then be very sure that you're leaving for the right reason. Not to punish Cole. Not to make him feel the weight of what he's about to lose. But because you truly can't stay." She paused. "Can you?"

Sydney pulled her hands free, pressed her fingertips to her eyes. She would not cry again. She had cried enough to last her the entire flight to London.

"Staying means seeing him every day," she said. "It means working for him. It means watching him get over it—or not—from ten feet away. I can't do that."

Renata nodded slowly. That was all. Just an understanding nod.

"Then go," Renata said. "And know that we love you. Know that this place loves you. And come back when you're ready."

Solana picked up the last box and settled it under her arm. "I'm taking this to your car." Her voice was even, practical, but she patted Sydney's shoulder on her way past, and then she was gone.

Sydney pressed her hand to her mouth. Renata opened her arms. She stepped into Renata's warm embrace. She'd miss her and Solana. Both were more like sisters than just friends.

"I'll call," Sydney said into her shoulder.

"You'd better." Renata pulled back and looked at her, just for a moment, the way only someone who had prayed with you through the hard things could. "Now go say goodbye to Madison before I make you stay."

Sydney picked up her purse and walked out.

She loaded the last of her boxes into her car, then sat behind the wheel without starting it. The desert beyond the fence line stretched wide and indifferent under the midday sun. She'd watched that view from her window more mornings than she could count.

She started the car.

The ranch road wound north, past the dining hall, past the sports complex. She kept her eyes forward and her hands steady on the wheel. When the big house came into view and the row of custom homes beyond it, she slowed and pulled into Madison and Derin's drive.

She knocked on Madison's door.

It opened before the sound finished.

"I saw your car." Madison's eyes were already red-rimmed. She stepped back to let Sydney in, and the familiar warmth of the house settled around her. The comfy furniture, the soft rugs, and the smell of something Chef had probably sent over that morning. Madison had always known how to make a space feel lived-in. Sydney had tried to learn from her.

Derin stood in the kitchen doorway with his coffee mug and a deep scowl.

"He's an idiot," he said.

"Derin." Madison's tone held a warning.

"I'm just saying." He looked at Sydney, and his jaw tightened. "She doesn't have to go."

"Derin." Madison jabbed him in the ribs with her elbow.

He absorbed it without flinching. "I said what I said."

Sydney laughed despite herself. "Thank you. I think."

He pushed off the door frame and crossed the room and hugged her once, quick and solid, and then stepped back and looked at the ceiling like something there required his full attention.

Madison took her hands the same way Renata had, but where Renata had been steady, Madison was barely holding herself together. Her eyes brimmed. She blinked. Lost the battle.

"You were supposed to be here forever," she said. "You know that, right? That was the plan."

"I know."

"Be an honorary auntie to little Maverick."

Sydney snorted. "Please don't name her that."

"Oh, if it's a girl, we won't. But a boy?" Madison hooked her thumb over her shoulder and rolled her eyes. "He won."

"I'll come back for a visit."

Madison sniffed. "The plan was that Cole would finally get his act together, and you'd move about twelve minutes off the ranch, and we'd have Sunday dinners forever, and our kids would grow up together and—"

"Madi." Derin's voice cut through the litany right as Madison's voice broke.

She pressed her lips together and shook her head. "Sorry. Sorry, I'm making this about me. I know, I know."

Madison pulled Sydney into a hug that rivaled Renata's, her arms wrapped tightly. Sydney's eyes burned and the words stuck in her throat. Those had been her dreams too.

"I love you. You're one of my favorite people on this earth. And you are always, always welcome here." Madison pulled back just enough to look at Sydney's face. "For a visit. For an extended stay." She held her gaze. "Or forever."

"I know," she whispered at last.

Madison hugged her again. Over her shoulder, Sydney could see Derin still studying the ceiling. His jaw worked once.

She'd built a family here. People who would fight for her no matter what.

It was almost the life she'd always wanted. Just one person missing.

And that was why she had to leave.

The thought followed her all the way to her car. It followed her down the ranch road and through the gate, past the sports complex where she'd spent a year building something she loved, past the turn toward where Cole's house sat quiet in the midday sun. She kept her eyes on the road.

Like the widow of Zarephath, she gathered her sticks, dropping off her boxes and car at the shipping company. A rideshare took her toward the airport, the desert opening wide on either side, saguaros standing their patient vigil in the heat.

You don't want to leave.

She knew. She knew she didn't.

The widow had gathered her sticks, not knowing what came next. Sydney knew exactly what came next. A flat in London that was neither new nor home, a job, a life that looked nothing like the one she'd planned. No miracle. Just the long road ahead.

But she went anyway.

12

COLE HAD MADE a strategic error.

He'd said yes to Derin without asking exactly what an offsite executive leadership meeting entailed. He'd assumed it meant some light observation from the shade of a palo verde. He should have known. With Derin, it always came back to cattle.

He was wrong.

"You're doing great." Derin's grin said otherwise.

"I'm dying." Cole shifted in the saddle and regretted it immediately. Every muscle from the waist down had staged a protest around the first hour. They were now well into hour three.

The August sun had no mercy. It pressed down on the back of his neck like a brand, turning the air above the scrub brush into something that shimmered. The herd moved slowly ahead of them, a few dozen head drifting toward the tank on the far side of the pasture. Dust rose off the ground in pale columns. It coated the inside of Cole's mouth, settled in his collar, and worked its way into the creases of his knuckles.

He was going to need to throw away this shirt.

"You know," Derin said, riding beside him—like the horse and the heat and the work were all as easy as breathing—"most guys loosen up a little the third time they do this."

"I've done this exactly twice. Counting today."

"That tracks."

The horse beneath Cole—a patient bay named Domino that Ross had selected with thinly veiled pity—plodded forward without complaint. At least one of them was handling this with dignity. Cole pressed his free hand against the small of his back and straightened.

"How are you not melting?"

Derin squinted out at the herd. "You get used to it."

"This is my second summer here."

"In an air-conditioned office." He glanced over, not unkind. "Not the same, bro."

Cole couldn't argue that. He'd always been drawn to the rhythm of ranch life—the slower pace than LA, the way time moved differently out here. The sense that the land had been here long before anyone's agenda. He'd just never been particularly interested in the sweat component.

Sydney would love this. The thought arrived without warning. He could picture it perfectly—her perched on the fence rail with a bottle of water and that look she got when she was trying not to laugh, watching him saddle-sore and sun-scorched while Derin rode circles around him. She'd have kept a straight face for maybe thirty seconds.

Cole exhaled slowly and fixed his eyes on the horizon.

Ahead, the herd gathered at the water tank, cattle pressing together, indifferent and slow and entirely unbothered by the heat. A hawk circled above, riding the thermals. The mountains in the distance had gone hazy blue with distance and heat shimmer.

He'd thought, when he first moved to Vargas Ranch, that the landscape would feel barren. It didn't. It felt like honesty. Everything stripped down to exactly what it was.

Lately, that felt appropriate.

"Pastor Jared thinks I'm making progress." Cole said it to the horizon, not to Derin.

"You agree?" Derin had known about the counseling sessions since the week Cole started.

"I think I finally understand what I actually did wrong." He shifted in the saddle again, this time out of restlessness rather than discomfort.

Derin waited. That was one thing Cole had always valued about him. He didn't fill the silence.

"I should have told Sydney about Audrey the night I knew where things were going between us. Before it got serious. Not after fourteen months." He paused. "I told myself I was protecting her. Really, I was protecting my brokenness."

"Yeah," Derin said.

"Pastor's been walking me through the difference between burying my brokenness versus confronting it." Cole's jaw tightened briefly. "Turns out I had the concept completely backwards. Burying something isn't the same as forgetting it. It's just hiding it somewhere dark and hoping it doesn't come back up."

"It always comes back up."

"Every time." He rubbed the back of his neck, dislodging a line of sweat. "I buried the guilt about my marriage, and it came back up every time I tried to get close to Sydney. Every time I tried to propose. It was always right there."

A cow at the edge of the herd drifted, and Derin's horse moved before Derin visibly asked it to. The animal redirected without drama. Derin circled back.

"We'll make a cowboy out of you yet, Gregory."

"Please don't."

The faintest edge of a smile pulled at Cole's mouth. He had smiled little lately. It felt strange. Not wrong, exactly. Just like something he'd have to relearn.

He felt the new thing God was doing in his heart, mind, and soul.

He just didn't know if it was too late.

That was the part he couldn't resolve, no matter how

many sessions he sat through or how many miles he covered in early morning prayer. He'd damaged something and it might not be fixable. Sydney had walked out of his house with her keys in her hand and he hadn't stopped her, because she'd been right to go.

She'd built a life here, trusting him. She deserved better than what he'd given her.

The memory surfaced the way they always did out here—when his hands were occupied and his mind had nothing to do but run. Carlino's. The Italian place on Tegner that had opened about six months into their relationship, still working out its operation. Sydney had found it on some local food blog and declared they had to try it.

The clearly new waiter had taken their order with exacting care and returned twenty minutes later with the wrong food.

Cole had reached for someone to flag down. Sydney caught his arm.

"Wait." Her eyes were already alight. "What'd you get?"

He looked at the plate. "Lasagna. I ordered the salmon."

"I got chicken parm. I ordered the lasagna." She was grinning. "Trade me."

"Sydney—"

"Cole." She'd slid his plate toward her and pushed the chicken parmesan across the table before he could finish the thought. "Enjoy the surprise. When else does a date night come with a mystery entrée?"

He'd eaten it. Under protest, at least nominally. The first bite was fine. By the end of the plate, he was reconsidering his entire relationship with Italian food, and Sydney had eaten her lasagna with encouraging words to him about the chicken parmesan. Gushing over the bite he'd shared with her.

She had been exactly right. The chicken parmesan at Carlino's was the best thing he'd ever had at a restaurant that cost under forty dollars a plate, a discovery he never would have made if she hadn't talked him out of flagging down the waiter.

They'd gone back the next month. And the month after that. Cole always ordered the chicken parmesan now. The waiter, now more confident, less nervous, always brought it without being asked.

He'd been back twice since she left. Alone. Ordered the chicken parmesan both times.

The food was still good. But it wasn't the same.

Nothing was the same.

Domino plodded on beneath him patiently. The herd was settling down. Derin pulled up alongside him again, and they rode the last stretch in silence.

Pastor Jared had helped him see himself as he was. Not with condemnation, but with the grace and wisdom of a man of God. "The things we bury don't disappear. They just grow in the dark until they break the surface. Things brought into the light—God's light—start to heal."

He could not undo what he'd done to Sydney.

What he could control was the man he was becoming on the other side of it. And he was not finished yet. The peace that came after surrendering still surprised him.

Derin brought his horse to a stop at the fence line and studied him.

"You're going to be okay," he said. Not a question.

Cole looked out at the mountains. "Working on it."

Derin nodded once.

The hawk above them banked wide and caught a current, riding it until it was just a dark point against the white-hot sky, and then it was gone. Cole watched the spot where it had been for a long moment.

He figured he owed Derin at least today. Maybe a few more days after that. His friend hadn't said a word about the fact that he'd kept the secret from him. Hadn't demanded an accounting. That first week after Sydney left, he'd shown up at Cole's house with a casserole Madison made and sat with him until it stopped feeling like the walls were caving in.

"Same time next week?" Derin asked.

Cole looked at the saddle. His back. The dust coated everything he owned.

"No, thanks?"

"Next quarter it is." Derin's grin broke wide. "We'll make a cowboy out of you yet."

"You said that already."

"Still true."

Cole resettled his hat against the sun and turned Domino back toward the barn. The afternoon heat pressed down, relentless and indifferent, and his entire lower half would hate him tomorrow.

He kinda liked a day in nature, clearing his head. Even if it made it hard to walk like a normal human for a few days.

SYDNEY WATCHED FROM the shade next to the stands as Luca opened the match without hesitation, the first point his before his opponent had fully settled.

She had twenty minutes with nothing to fill them but her own thoughts.

She eased into her seat just off the player box and tucked the water bottle his trainer had handed her under her arm. The stadium noise rolled over her in waves—not the sharp burst-and-lull of American sports crowds, but a continuous murmur that lifted and fell with each point. The hard court blazed blue-green under the afternoon light.

At first, the energy of the sport felt familiar, welcoming even. Until around the third week, when the numb routine of it took hold and the ache for Vargas Ranch started.

Luca moved into position for the next serve, the movement fluid. She'd watched him play enough times over the years—first from the edges of Madison's world, then courtside here—to know he was locked in. His opponent made minor adjustments, but the gentle slump in his shoulders projected defeat.

Luca was a good boss. Easygoing with genuine confidence. Not too demanding. He didn't make the job harder than it was. She'd appreciated that from the start.

She just hadn't expected to feel this hollow doing it.

Sydney pulled out her phone and skimmed through the morning's messages. A photo from Renata—something about a birthday cake for one kid from the equine therapy program, frosting in improbable colors. A voice memo from Madison that was forty-seven seconds long, which meant it was either very funny or a pregnancy update, or both. Sydney would listen to it on the way back to the hotel.

She missed them.

She'd known she would. She thought it would get easier with time.

Renata would be baking this morning. Sydney knew it the way she knew the ranch schedule by heart. Tuesday meant the kitchen in their apartment smelled like cinnamon and brown sugar before the sun was fully up, and whoever wandered in got handed something warm without being asked.

She'd missed the soup kitchen in Wickenburg again yesterday. Second month in a row. She and Solana had gone every month for a year, showing up early, working the line together, staying after to stack chairs and mop floors and talk the way you only talked when your hands were busy doing something useful. Sydney had loved those mornings. Serving alongside someone who didn't need to fill every silence. Bringing joy to the hungry and homeless.

She still hadn't listened to the voice memo on her phone from Madison. Forty-seven seconds. Sydney's thumb hovered over it. She'd listen to it on the way back to the hotel, when she could give it her full attention. When she could hear Madison's voice and not be in the middle of a crowd where crying would require explanation.

Madison was due in December. Four months away. Sydney had done the math more than once, measuring the tournament calendar against the due date, calculating the gap between where she'd likely be and where she desperately wanted to be. Courtside at some indoor hard court in November. Not in Arizona, holding her best friend's hand.

She'd assumed, somewhere in the foggy reasoning of packing up and buying plane tickets, that distance would help. That the missing would dull as Europe filled the space where Vargas Ranch had been.

Instead, the space got bigger.

Home used to mean Iowa. The flat horizon and the particular smell of rain on field corn and the way her mother kept the house too warm from October through March. She'd left Iowa at twenty-two and looked back exactly once, and even then it hadn't pulled at her the way she'd expected.

Home had changed somewhere along the way. She hadn't noticed the exact moment it happened. Just one day she'd caught herself thinking how desperately she wanted to go home and realized she'd meant the ranch.

Possibly meant a certain blue-eyed cowboy-hat-wearing COO too.

She pressed her fingers to the side of her water bottle and watched the court.

A point ended badly on the next court over. The player—young, ranked in the eighties, clearly having a terrible afternoon—sat down at the changeover with her head tipped back and her eyes closed. Her coach crouched in front of her, talking. She shook her head. The coach kept talking.

A man appeared at the edge of Sydney's vision. Not a coach. Volunteer staff of some kind, or press, or someone involved with the tournament in a capacity she didn't recognize. He made his way to the young player, and the coach stepped back slightly. The man crouched down in the same way the coach had. Then he took both the player's hands in his. Bowed his head.

The player's shoulders dropped. Not defeat—something else. An exhale that meant someone had just told her she didn't have to carry it alone.

Sydney's throat tightened.

The memory came the way they always did now. Poignantly. Drawing her heart away from her present space.

She'd been four months into dating Cole, and she'd been early to a meeting at the sports complex. She'd come down the back corridor and turned the corner, and there he was—in the main room off to the side, standing with an athlete from a rehabilitation program. A football player, she thought, though she hadn't caught the name. Young. Early in his career. Cole had his back to Sydney, and she hadn't been able to hear the words over the ambient noise of the building.

But she'd seen it. The way Cole had stood—not rushed, not checking his phone, or angled toward the door. Present in a way she'd occasionally see him in a professional setting instead of his usual motion, already three steps into the next thing. His hand had been on the young man's shoulder. His head slightly bowed. Later she learned the athlete had given his life to Christ.

She'd turned around and walked back the way she'd come, and she hadn't said a word to Cole about it. But she'd carried it back to her office and set it down carefully somewhere in her heart where important things lived.

That was the moment she knew. She wanted Cole Gregory as her husband. As the father of her children.

Sydney sniffed and blinked her eyes rapidly.

The ache was old and as visceral as that day. No matter what had happened between them, she couldn't stop loving him. No distance, no mistake on his part or hers, could lessen that love. She'd quietly forgiven him a few days ago. And that had only led to a greater longing.

On the court, Luca took the second set with little effort. The crowd offered a warm roar. His opponent looked weary. Luca acknowledged the applause with a brief raise of his racket and walked back to the baseline.

She pressed her fingertips against the cross at her throat, the metal smooth and slightly warmed by the sun.

She'd taken it off once, her first night in London. Held it in her palm under the hotel lamp for a long time. The gift instead of the ring. Now it had become the piece of him she'd carried across an ocean, resting so close to her heart. Day after day, she couldn't leave it in a drawer.

Maybe that meant something. She wasn't sure what.

There had been a night early on—a long layover in a terminal somewhere between one city and the next, three in the morning local time. She had been so tired the edges of things went soft. She'd pulled out her phone, and the verse had surfaced, present and immediate. *I sought the Lord, and he answered me, and rescued me from all my fears.* She'd saved it. Come back to it more times than she could count since.

She'd been waiting for Cole to be ready. Waiting for a commitment on the timeline she'd decided was appropriate. Waiting for five almost-proposals and praying for the one that was the beginning of their forever. What she hadn't been doing was waiting on God. There was a difference. She understood that now in a way she hadn't when she'd packed her boxes.

She wasn't afraid anymore. Not of Cole, or his failures. Not of what she didn't know. Not of the future, sitting dark and unresolved on the horizon. The fear had loosened its grip somewhere over the Atlantic, and the thing left behind wasn't certainty. Just a quiet that felt like trust.

She didn't have to see the full plan. She just had to trust the One holding it.

Luca opened the third set, efficient and unhurried, like a man with a long afternoon planned and nothing to worry about. Sydney gathered her mindset back to the job. Her notes. His schedule. The two calls she needed to make before six.

She was good at this. That part hadn't changed.

She had walked back into the rhythm of it—the noise and the work and the forward motion of a tournament day—with the cross resting at her throat. One day this would make sense.

She believed that now.

13

COLE GREGORY HAD been to New York more times than he could count. He'd tried to count them once, on a red-eye back to LAX with a client contract signed and a migraine forming behind his left eye. Some where around thirty he lost count. He knew which coffee shop at JFK had the best coffee before six in the morning and which car services were worth the surcharge. He knew the particular weight of Manhattan air in August—thick and unapologetic about exactly what it was.

He was not a man who got rattled by New York.

He was, however, a man in Lucchese boots walking through the USTA Billie Jean King National Tennis Center with a ring box in his front shirt pocket, which was a first.

Cole had taken his new Tahoe to Sky Harbor. Left the McLaren in the garage under its cover, climate-controlled, the way a car like that deserved to be kept. It was a beautiful machine, and he wasn't pretending otherwise. He'd just grabbed the other keys without deliberating, backed out of the driveway, knowing Sydney would like the new SUV. No second-guessing behind it.

Three days ago, he'd heard Derin's truck in the driveway before the knock. He opened the door and Madison stood on the step, one hand resting on her belly.

She scanned the room, studied him, and blurted out,

"You look terrible."

"I'm aware."

She walked past him into the kitchen without waiting for an invitation, Derin a step behind her. They'd brought takeout from the Italian place on Tegner. Carlino's. Cole stood in the doorway to his own kitchen, watching Madison set containers on the table.

Derin pulled out a chair and sat.

"Sit down," he said. Not a suggestion.

Cole sat.

For a few minutes, nobody said anything important. Madison dished up a plate for Cole and herself. Derin served himself. Cole ate without tasting much.

Then Madison reached into her bag and set the ring box on the table next to his fork.

Cole went still.

"Derin found it," she said. Her voice was even. "It doesn't belong in a desk drawer."

He picked it up. Turned it in his hand. The velvet was worn at one corner—months in a jacket pocket would do that. He'd stopped carrying it after Sydney left. Couldn't look at it.

Derin set down his fork.

"You've done the work," he said. "I've watched you do it. Pastor Jared, counseling every week." He leaned forward, elbows on the table. "Now do the hard part."

"The hard part," Cole said.

"Go get her!" Madison exclaimed throwing her hands in the air. She'd been edgier in her second trimester. Even he'd noticed.

Cole turned the box over in his hands again. The worn corner. The hinge that still opened cleanly.

"What if she—"

"She loves you," Madison said. "I hear it every time she asks about you. Which is every time we talk."

Cole looked up.

"She asks about me?"

Madison gave him the look that meant he was being slow on purpose. "Cole."

Derin pushed back from the table and walked to the hallway. When he came back several minutes later, he carried a suitcase. He set it on the floor next to Cole's chair.

"Madi can't go to the US Open."

"I could. The doctor said—"

Derin scowled at his wife.

She huffed. "Overbearing."

"Protective. It's my job."

Cole held back a smirk, used to their dynamic.

"You're going to miss your flight," she said. "Finish your dinner and then go."

"What flight?"

Derin reached into his back pocket and placed a printed boarding pass on the table.

Cole picked it up. New York. Red-eye out of Sky Harbor.

For years, he'd flown dozens of red-eyes. Sometimes trying to get back to California to smooth over a problem with Audrey. Others just so he could spend a full twenty-four hours in his apartment—after the divorce—to feel like he belonged somewhere before heading out again.

Always making deals. Securing his clients' futures.

Now this boarding pass meant securing his future.

Those five failed proposals rose to his mind. Christmas. Valentine's Day. The most devastating of all—her birthday, where he'd had the gall to blame her. Five times he'd gotten close and let fear win.

Fear was a liar. Pastor Jared had said that. Cole had written it down and stared at it for two months before he believed it.

He believed it now.

He put the boarding pass in his shirt pocket. Then the ring box on top of it.

Derin watched him. Something in his expression—not quite a smile, but close.

"I did the same thing to you once," Cole said.

"I know."

"You drove through a snowstorm in a Prius."

Derin chuckled. "Barely fit."

Cole exhaled. Picked up his fork. "The chicken parmesan is good here."

"I know that too," Derin said. "Sydney told Madison."

Cole ate the rest of his dinner before hopping into his shiny new Tahoe—a family vehicle Madison called it—leaving behind the flashy McLaren and the too-expensive Ram TRX. He'd made it to the airport with plenty of time to get through security.

The red-eye lifted out of Sky Harbor at eleven forty-two. Cole had the window seat. He'd always taken the aisle on business trips because it was easier to move, easier to work, and easier to be ready for whatever came next.

Tonight he wanted the window.

He watched the Phoenix grid drop away beneath him, the city lights spreading wide and then giving way to the dark sweep of desert. Somewhere down there was Vargas Ranch. A house with an empty fruit bowl on the counter. A life he was finally building instead of just occupying.

He opened his Bible app. Found Isaiah 43. Pastor Jared had brought it up in their third session, almost offhand. "No matter how long you've walked with God, He can still do a new thing in you."

Cole had been a believer since high school. He'd assumed that meant he'd already been made new. That the transformation happened at salvation and the rest was just maintenance.

He'd been wrong about that.

The counseling had shown him what he'd buried instead of grieved. The end of his marriage to Audrey hadn't just been a failure he'd packed away; it was a loss he'd never faced head-on. Hadn't ever really dealt with the lies he'd let take root in his heart about himself.

He'd moved cities, changed careers, built new walls around the wound and called it healing.

Pastor Jared had called it avoidance.

Cole had not enjoyed that session.

But somewhere between then and this boarding pass, something had shifted. Not fixed. He wasn't naïve enough to think a few months of honest conversation undid years of hiding.

Behold, I am doing a new thing. Do you not perceive it?

He felt the new thing God was doing in his heart, mind, and soul.

He put his phone away and leaned his head back. For the first time in longer than he could measure, he wasn't managing anything. Wasn't fixing a mistake or filling twenty-four hours in a city for a client's future hopes.

He was going toward something. Someone.

His own future, finally, with the woman he couldn't live without.

He slept the rest of the way to JFK.

Now, at the US Open, he moved through the player access corridor with the calm authority of someone who had navigated a hundred venues like this one. Badge clipped. Hat adjusted. The beard had thickened through the summer—fuller than anything he'd worn in his agent days, when image was his currency. His managing partner had once told him to shave before a contract meeting because old money wanted smooth chins. Cole had shaved.

He didn't miss it.

The corridor opened into the main stadium concourse, and the crowd noise lifted, rolling up off concrete and glass and open sky. He knew this sound. Knew the particular pitch of a US Open afternoon crowd.

He'd stood in spaces like this for more than a decade with a phone in one hand and a contract in the other. Working the edges. Running to the next thing, the next deal, the next call. Always three steps ahead of where he was standing.

Cole stopped at the rail and looked down. He'd stood at rails like this one for years. Different venues, different coasts, different clients below. Always scanning for the angle, the opportunity, the next move. He'd been good at it. He'd been very good at it.

That version of himself felt like a different man entirely.

Below him, the match was deep in the final set. The crowd had pulled in on itself, breath held, the noise dropping to something low and electric. He'd felt that energy a hundred times and never once let himself just be inside it.

He let himself stand still.

The first thing that caught his attention was her hair catching the afternoon light. Spine straight. The sight of her hit him the way water hits parched ground after a brutal stretch without rain.

She turned slightly, one hand resting near her collarbone. The cross pendant caught a flash of sun.

The intricate vine around the cross symbolized his love for God and for her. The roses represented her beauty in his eyes. She didn't know the full meaning behind the design. He'd tell her soon.

That she wore it even now—even knowing the giving had been delivered poorly. Timed all wrong.

Cole's hand went to his shirt pocket as he stepped toward the stairs.

She still hadn't seen him. She was watching the match. Doing her job well. Fully present. She'd always been present. Even when he hadn't been.

He reached the lower level and came around the outside of the section. Twenty yards. Fifteen. His Lucchese boots on concrete, ring box in his palm now, the velvet worn soft at one corner.

A woman somewhere behind him, half-whisper: "Is that

Cole Gregory?"

A second voice: "He looks like a cowboy."

He didn't look back.

She was ten yards ahead, still unaware, the cross at her throat catching the light.

Peace settled into him. Solid. Sure.

Then he closed the distance between him and his almost wife.

THREE DAYS AGO, Madison had called at eleven at night.

Sydney had been sitting on the edge of her hotel bed, shoes still on, too tired to take them off after a match that ran four and a half hours. Outside the window, New York glittered as if it had no idea what exhaustion was.

"I miss you," Sydney said before Madison could even get through hello.

Madison's laugh was warm and familiar and entirely too far away. "Then come home."

"After the US Open." Sydney pulled off one shoe, then the other. "Tell me something from home. Anything."

Madison obliged. She relayed a funny story about Derin refusing to pick a girl's name. "He's positive we are having a boy… And he's right, but I just don't want to tell him yet. I kinda want him to feel the pressure."

Sydney laughed. "A boy. Maverick then?"

Madison sighed. "Yeah."

"Tell me what Chef made for dinner. And which Vargas brother do you think will get married next?"

While Madison answered, Sydney closed her eyes and let herself be homesick in full.

"How are you, really?" Madison asked.

"Tired." The truest answer.

A pause. "Derin won't let me fly." Madison's voice carried its own brand of frustration. "Doctor's orders. I am so sorry I can't be there."

"I know." Sydney pulled her knees to her chest. "It's okay."

"It's not, and we both know that." Another pause, shorter. "But I'm sending someone."

"Who?"

"Nope." Sydney could hear the smile. "You'll know when they get there."

Sydney had assumed it was Renata. Or maybe Solana. Some piece of home wrapped in a friendly face, showing up to help her cheer Luca across the finish line.

But a tiny corner of her heart hoped… She shook her head. No use going there.

She'd find out tomorrow.

The next morning, Sydney's alarm was set for six-fifteen, but she woke before it. Gray light at the window. She'd slept fitfully. Madison's words looped through her head all night. She'd told herself it was Renata. Possibly Solana.

Her heart hadn't believed her.

She pressed her fingers to the cross at her throat. The metal was warm from sleep.

She'd thought leaving Vargas Ranch was the end of her waiting. That was what she'd told herself when she packed up her things, loaded her car, and said goodbye to Renata and Solana in the living room. She'd done the hard thing. She'd stopped waiting and moved forward. That was supposed to be the end of it.

But here she was. Still waiting. Just from a different city.

Pastor Jared's voice surfaced, quiet and unhurried, the way it had that Sunday in the sanctuary. *We can't see what is on the other side of waiting. But He still asks us to wait. To trust.*

She'd thought she understood that then. Maybe she hadn't. Maybe she was still learning it.

The alarm went off. She silenced it, pushed back the covers, and got up. She carried that hope with her all morning, fragile as it was, through the US Open credentials check, the walk to the player area, and the familiar rituals of a tournament day. By the time Luca took the court for the final, she'd almost talked herself out of it.

Almost.

The crowd hushed behind her. Luca was on serve, up a break in the final set, and the stadium held its breath. Sydney tracked the ball without thinking, the old muscle memory of a thousand similar afternoons.

He'd been extraordinary in this tournament. She'd told him so that morning, and he'd said, "Extraordinary assistants produce extraordinary tennis," with the cheerful arrogance that made him absolutely insufferable and somehow still endearing. She told him he could find his own snacks next time. He'd pretended to be devastated.

Luca wound up. Served. His opponent's return sailed wide.

The crowd erupted.

Sydney let out a breath and grinned despite herself. A murmur started somewhere behind her, just below the noise, the particular low current of recognition that moved through a crowd when someone unexpected walked in. She half-turned to look, but the cheering swelled again, and the moment passed, and Luca was raising his racket to the sky with a grin wide enough to be seen from the upper deck.

She turned back to the court.

He'd done it. Eight months of brutal work, a career on the line, and Luca Marchetti had earned his way back to the top of the draw. She'd done her job well. And she was proud of his work.

But that incessant pull back to Arizona, to Vargas Ranch, refused to lift, even while celebrating her boss's success.

The crowd noise shifted to the lower roar of conclusion, the shuffle and movement of people beginning to go. Luca headed for the tunnel, and Sydney straightened, rolling her shoulders, already cataloging the next three hours of post-match logistics.

She turned, and her breath caught.

"Cole?"

Her brain registered the familiar form in a charcoal-gray sports coat. Black Lucchese boots. Tom Ford denim. Dark cowboy hat. Blue eyes sparkling. Grin fading as he strode toward her.

Somewhere in the rows behind her, a woman gasped. Then another. A ripple of murmurs, and then—as his hand opened the box—a collective intake of breath that had nothing to do with tennis.

Then he dropped to one knee, his impossibly handsome, beard-covered face filling her vision.

He clasped her hand in his.

"You're here?" she asked.

"Sydney Steele." His voice didn't waver. Not even a little. "I have practiced that sentence approximately four hundred times, and I still can't believe I get to say it." A breath. "I know what I cost you. I know what the waiting took. I know I owe you honesty I should have given you from the start, and a ring I should have put on your finger nine months ago, and a home I should have been brave enough to build." His hand tightened around hers. "I am done being afraid. I am done with being your almost fiancé. You are the only woman I have ever wanted a future with, and I want it right now, all of it, for the rest of my life. So please, will you forgive me and will you marry me?"

The ring glinted from the little box, a round stone in a white gold setting with small diamonds trailing down each side. Perfect. Absolutely, unreservedly him.

"Yes," she said, and launched herself at him.

He caught her, arms wrapping around her before she could second-guess the physics of two people colliding beside a tennis court. The sound that came out of her was something between a laugh and a sob, and she didn't particularly care which. She pressed her face into his neck. He was warm and solid and he smelled like Cole, like home, and her whole body went loose with it, the long months of ache releasing all at once.

That's when the cheering started. Not the polished roar of a match point—something warmer, more ragged, the sound of strangers deciding to be happy for two people they'd never meet.

"Yes," she said again, into his collar, quieter this time. For her. For him.

"Thank you," he murmured into her hair.

Somewhere behind them, a slow clap started. One pair of hands. Italian accent, thoroughly amused.

"Bravissimo," Luca said. "I did not expect my post-match entertainment to include this, but I am not complaining."

Sydney laughed, still in Cole's arms. She turned her head just enough to look at Luca, who stood with his arms folded and his expression set to a particular mixture of magnanimity and inconvenience.

Cole kissed her then, and Luca apparently decided he had other places to be.

When the kiss ended, Cole took her hand and steered them toward the corridor that wrapped the outside of the court, out of the foot traffic and the noise, and back toward something quieter.

"Hey, Luca!" she called over her shoulder.

He paused. Looked back.

"I quit. I'm going home."

She turned and followed Cole.

They found a corner near a service entrance, concrete walls and a flickering fluorescent above the door, glamorous by absolutely no measure. Cole didn't let go of her hand.

"I should have told you about Audrey the day it became relevant," he said. No preamble. "I should have trusted you."

"You should have," she agreed. No softening to it, but

no edge either. "I needed the real you, Cole. Not the version you thought I could handle."

He nodded. His thumb traced a slow line across her knuckles. "I know."

She looked at his face—the exhaustion under his eyes, the set of his jaw, and the way he stood like a man who'd spent months putting himself back together. She'd done the same.

"I forgive you." She said with no buildup. "I forgave you a while ago. I just needed time to fully hand it over to God."

Something moved behind his eyes. He exhaled slowly, and the line of his shoulders dropped an inch.

"I love you," he said. "I have loved you since that Tuesday when you handed me the wrong office key and then apologized so many times I lost count."

She shook her head. "That was embarrassing."

"It was perfect." He cupped her face with both hands. "You were perfect. Are perfect."

The second kiss was nothing like the first. Quieter. Steadier. Full of every dream they'd made together.

When he pulled back, one corner of his mouth quirked.

"Unrelated," he said, "but how do you feel about getting married today?"

Sydney stared at him.

"There's a chapel," he offered. "I looked it up."

"Cole."

"Or Pastor Jared can do it over video—"

She kissed him again, which was not technically an answer, but from the way he laughed against her mouth, he didn't seem to mind.

Epilogue

SYDNEY DIDN'T MOVE right away.

No alarm. No itinerary she'd looked up the night before. No mental checklist of Luca's pre-match preferences pulled her out of bed before she was ready. Just the slow, easy drift toward consciousness and the particular warmth of her husband sleeping beside her.

Her husband.

A month, and she still hadn't gotten used to saying it. She suspected she never would, and that was perfectly fine with her.

Cole lay on his stomach, one arm stretched toward her side of the bed, face turned away. His breathing was deep and even. Outside the window of the rental, the Arizona sky had shifted from black to the pale gold that came just before sunrise, and the light falling across the bedroom floor was exactly what she'd described on that trail ride years ago. Slow. Quiet. Sunlight easing through the window as if it had nowhere else to be.

A lot had happened since that trail ride.

Four weeks ago she'd been standing beside a tennis court in New York with a brand new ring on her finger, laughing into Cole's collar while thirty thousand strangers cheered. Her engagement was short-lived. Cole had called Pastor Jared from a corridor near a service entrance, phone pressed to one ear, the particular calm confidence he used in contract negotiations firmly in place. Pastor Jared had laughed for a solid thirty seconds. Then he'd said yes.

They got married the following afternoon over a Zoom call that froze twice and dropped audio once. Pastor Jared stood in his office at the church in a button-down he'd clearly just ironed. Derin stood to his left, looking like a man trying very hard to hold himself together. Madison stood to his right, hands folded over the swell of her pregnancy, tears streaming freely down her face with zero apology. Sydney had worn the white sundress she and Cole had spotted in a Madison Avenue shop window that morning—he'd looked at it and said "that one" with a certainty that left no room for debate—and she'd carried a small bunch of white roses the hotel concierge had bought on forty minutes' notice.

When Pastor Jared pronounced them husband and wife, Derin made a sound that was half laugh and half something he'd never in a million years admit to, and Madison pressed both hands over her mouth, and the Zoom connection froze on a single frame of all four of them.

She still had the screenshot saved on her phone.

They'd stayed in New York three more days, and Luca had accepted her permanent resignation with theatrical devastation and entirely genuine warmth, pressing both her hands between his and promising, hand over heart, to ship everything from the London flat himself. She believed him. He was insufferable about most things, but he kept his word.

Then they'd come home to Arizona, signed papers on a house that the realtor had described, almost apologetically, as a touch large for two people—four bedrooms, a yard backing up to open desert, a kitchen with more counter space than any reasonable couple could use—and Cole had looked at her over the realtor's head with one eyebrow slightly raised and she had nodded, and they'd made an offer that afternoon.

They closed on it yesterday.

Today they were moving.

She lay still for another full minute, cataloging the sounds of the rental for the last time. The refrigerator hummed. A neighbor's dog barked in the distance. The faint tick of the house settling in the cool October air.

Cole stirred. Turned his head. Opened one eye.

"Morning," he said, voice rough with sleep.

"Moving day," she said.

He closed the eye again. "Give me five minutes."

"Adan will be here in forty-five," she chided gently.

Sydney hopped out of bed and padded to the shower. By the time she'd dressed and started the coffee, Cole appeared in the kitchen, reaching past her for a mug, hair still damp. The sound of tires on the gravel drive announced that Adan had arrived early. Cole stole a quick kiss before he opened the door.

Adan parked his truck with the bed already loaded with flattened boxes and a thermos of coffee balanced on the passenger seat, Solana beside him with two dozen breakfast burritos from Chef stacked in a paper bag on her lap. Dylan and Brisa pulled in behind them before Sydney had finished her first cup. Parker arrived with Ross, both in worn work gloves.

Derin parked his truck before rounding to the passenger side. Madison slid awkwardly to the ground with her husband's hands steadying her.

Derin pointed at her before she'd taken two steps. "Don't touch a thing, Madi."

"I can carry a box—"

"You can tape a box. Maybe."

"That's not—"

"Doctor's orders." He was already pulling boxes from the truck bed. "Go supervise."

Madison turned to Sydney with an expression of profound suffering. "He's been like this for three months."

"He's not wrong," Sydney said, lifting her coffee mug to

hide her smirk.

Madison's expression shifted to betrayal. "Et tu?"

Her best friend supervised magnificently. Standing in the center of whatever room needed organizing, one hand on her lower back, directing traffic with calm authority. When Ross and Parker carried Cole's couch through the front door and couldn't agree on which direction to turn it, Madison resolved the dispute in under ten seconds. When Dylan stacked boxes in the wrong order, she had Adan re-stack them before he made it back to the truck. Cole caught Sydney's eye across the living room and mouthed something that looked like "she's terrifying." Sydney pressed her lips together and looked away before she laughed out loud.

The rental packed up faster than she expected. When the last box was taped, Renata hugged her in the empty living room. "This is exactly what we prayed for."

Sydney nodded. Then she crossed to the last item. The empty fruit bowl. Cole had told her it was the last item he'd unpacked that day—the one she broke up with him. They'd decided to leave it empty, as a gentle reminder of what God had filled.

She lifted it carefully, set it in a box lined with dish towels, and wrote KITCHEN—HANDLE WITH CARE on top in black marker. Then she carried it to the Tahoe, tucking it carefully in the back.

By four o'clock the new house had been thoroughly invaded.

Furniture arranged and rearranged. Boxes were stacked in every room. Chef's green-chile chili simmered on the stove, the smell of it filling the kitchen. Solana had hauled it over in the back of her SUV so it would be ready when they arrived. They ate on the back porch as the sun dropped behind the desert hills, saguaros going dark against an orange sky, voices overlapping, someone's laugh carrying out across the yard.

Derin sat next to Madison, who finally sat after being

scolded no less than three times. Sydney loved their relationship. Funny how God could bring even a tennis pro and a bossy cowboy together.

Cole stood in the yard with Parker and Adan, clearly debating the outdoor furniture placement on the patio.

"They're going to move it again," Brisa said from the chair beside Sydney.

"Definitely," Sydney said. "As soon as we look away."

They watched Cole gesture decisively toward the left corner. Adan shook his head. Parker offered a third option. The furniture stayed where it was.

One by one the trucks pulled out as the stars came up, with hugs at the door and promises to return once pictures were hung and the kitchen was properly stocked. Derin pulled Cole in with one arm and said something low that Sydney didn't catch. Whatever it was made Cole nod slowly, the way he did when something landed true.

Madison held Sydney last.

"Welcome home," she whispered.

Sydney held on for an extra second before she let go.

The house went silent.

Cole found her in the kitchen, standing at the counter with a mug of decaf, looking out the window at the dark desert. He came and stood beside her, close enough that his shoulder pressed against hers, and said nothing for a while.

When she'd left Vargas Ranch for London, she'd thought leaving was the other side of the waiting. She understood now that it hadn't been.

This was.

She'd spent so much of the waiting assuming it was for her—that God was doing something in her heart, testing her faith. And when the waiting became too heavy, she left. Told herself it was the brave thing. The right thing.

Maybe God had been gracious enough to use her absence anyway to give Cole the space he needed, even when that hadn't been her intention at all.

The hardest part hadn't been the uncertainty about her own future. It had been loving Cole and knowing there was nothing she could do to help him. His journey had been his alone—between him and God. She could only wait and trust that God was working in him, even when she couldn't see it.

And God had. Cole had surrendered what he'd carried for years, done the quiet, unglamorous work of setting it down. She hadn't known to ask for that. Hadn't imagined that was what waited on the other side.

That was the miracle.

"We need to put something in that fruit bowl," Cole said.

Sydney glanced over her shoulder. There it was on the counter. Still empty.

She laughed, quiet and genuine, and leaned into him.

"Tomorrow," she said.

He pressed a kiss to the top of her head.

Outside, the desert settled into its nighttime silence, and the cool air wafted through the window screen.

Husband. Home.

Her reality was even better than the dream.

Author's Note

COLE GREGORY HAS lived in my imagination for a while now. First as the confident, driven businessman in *Falling for a Bossy Cowboy*, and then as the man I knew was hiding underneath all that polish. Writing his story in *Her Almost Fiancé Cowboy* gave me the chance to explore the heart of the man behind the facade.

Like Cole, I've walked through some hard seasons. I know what it's like to stuff pain down instead of processing it, to keep moving because stopping feels dangerous. It was important to me to show a strong Christian man—a man of genuine faith—who still needed to come to grips with his own grief. I learned long ago that Christ died to save me, not to make me perfect this side of heaven. Cole had to stop running long enough to let God meet him where he actually was, not where he thought he should be. Counseling became the gift that helped him see himself clearly, grieve honestly, and finally heal.

And Sydney? Her longing for roots is personal, too. My dad was in ministry, which meant our family moved—twice during my school years, including the middle of my junior year of high school. I grew up always being the new girl and always starting over. I wanted a place that felt like mine. Sydney's ache for belonging? I lived that. And just like her, as an adult, I found my people and built something that felt like home.

Shortly after I typed the last words of Cole and Sydney's story, I came across "The Day I Forgave Myself" by Storm Chant. I sat and listened to it several times, letting the words wash over me. Everything I'd just spent months writing was right there in that song. I've added it to the playlist for this series. Give it a listen when you're ready.

Spotify Playlist

https://open.spotify.com/playlist/19aPPgRlHDcwxe0LVXB4P5?si=BoR_Uz2iTwuje9xExp_sXA

If Cole and Sydney's journey left you wanting more Love at Vargas Ranch, Carter Wakefield's story is next. You met him briefly here. Now get ready to cheer for a rookie cowboy navigating life as a single dad after divorce in *Her Brave Rookie Cowboy.*

See you there!

Karen Baney

About the Author

Karen Baney is passionate about writing stories full of flawed characters. She enjoys weaving together stories of second chances, redemption, and overcoming personal trials. As a transplant to Arizona, she loves researching the state's history and finding ways to seamlessly incorporate real history and real settings into her novels. In addition to writing and speaking, Karen works as a Software Development Manager for a Christian ministry.

Her faith plays an important role both in her life and in her writing. Karen and her husband, Jim, make their home in Gilbert, Arizona, with their two dogs, Bella and Daisy. Both Jim and Karen are active at Rock Point Church in Queen Creek, Arizona.

Discover faith-laced stories with characters who feel like lifelong friends.

Visit www.karenbaney.com to discover more historical romance series set in the American West. Follow Karen's writing journey and get behind-the-scenes glimpses of her research adventures on social media.

Facebook: @AuthorKarenBaney
X: @karen_baney
Instagram: @AuthorKarenBaney
BookBub: Follow Karen Baney for new release alerts

Books By Karen Baney

Contemporary Romance

Vargas Ranch Series:

Love is in the air at the Vargas Guest Ranch & Resort near Wickenburg, Arizona. Meet the Vargas family—five swoon-worthy brothers and their cousins who live by their family motto: "We do not deviate from the Lord's plan." These rugged cowboys run a successful working ranch and luxury resort while navigating the rollercoaster of finding true love.

Falling for a Fake Cowboy
Falling for a Real Cowboy
Honeymoon with a Real Cowboy
Falling for a Shy Cowboy
Falling for a Bossy Cowboy
Falling for a Smart Cowboy
Falling for a Humbug Cowboy
Falling for a Devoted Cowgirl
Falling for a Pregnant Cowgirl
Falling for a Cowboy's Legacy

Love at Vargas Ranch Series

At a sprawling guest ranch near Wickenburg, Arizona, the series follows the hearts of hardworking cowboys, wranglers, and staff who keep the ranch alive. From equine therapy programs to trail rides under endless desert skies, each story brings together two wounded hearts longing for healing, hope, and love.

Her Mistaken Identity Cowboy
Her Almost Fiancé Cowboy

Her Brave Rookie Cowboy
Her Valentines Veteran Cowboy
More books planned

Steadfast Love Series:
The *Steadfast Love* series follows a close-knit group of friends as they navigate the beautiful mess of modern life in the Phoenix area—workplace drama, complicated families, and love that shows up when they least expect it. These contemporary romances blend emotional depth with authentic faith, reminding us that even when life unravels, God's love never does.

The Heart I Rescue (prequel)
The Air I Breathe

Historical Western Romance

Prescott Pioneers Series:
Step back in time to the wild, untamed Arizona Territory where survival depends on grit, faith, and the courage to start over. Follow three pioneer families—the Andersons, Colters, and Larsons—as they risk everything for the promise of a new life in a land that demands both strength and hope.

A Dream Unfolding
A Heart Renewed
A Life Restored
A Hope Revealed
Hidden Prospects

Desert Manna Series:
Sometimes the most beautiful love stories bloom in the desert. Set in the growing frontier town of Prescott during the early 1870s, these tender romances follow women rebuilding

their lives after heartbreak and the unexpected men who help them discover that second chances at love are worth the risk. Set in Prescott, Arizona between 1871 - 1873.

Beauty for Ashes
Joy for Mourning
Oaks of Justice

Colter Sons Series:

Power, legacy, and forbidden love collide in this sweeping family saga set in the Arizona Territory. The Colter ranch empire has weathered decades of frontier life, but now family secrets and buried betrayals threaten to destroy everything. As five brothers—and one resilient sister—navigate the treacherous waters of love, loss, and redemption, they must decide what's worth fighting for. Set in Prescott and other locations within the Arizona Territory in 1887 - 1906.

The Reluctant Cattleman
The Roaming Adventurer
The Railroad Magnate
The Resourceful Stockman
The Restless Wrangler
The Resilient Bride

Larson Sisters Series

Meet the next generation! These delightful novellas follow the three daughters of Adam and Julia Larson from the *Prescott Pioneers Series* as they navigate love, courtship, and finding their own happily ever afters in territorial Arizona in 1886 – 1894.

In Love at Christmas
In Love with the Rancher
In Love with the Horse Trainer

Desert Life Media

Desert Life Media: ***There Is Life in The Desert***

Entertainment-first Christian fiction set in the Southwest, featuring redemption, family, and faith

Publishing clean, wholesome, and uplifting fiction since 2010

---

desertlifemedia.com

www.ingramcontent.com/pod-product-compliance
Lightning Source LLC
LaVergne TN
LVHW010656110826
845149LV00014B/3121

* 9 7 8 1 9 6 0 2 1 7 7 7 6 *